CAPE MAY SNOWFLAKES

CLAUDIA VANCE

CHAPTER ONE

A crisp December breeze rustled the bare branches outside as Margaret stared out the kitchen window of their farmhouse in West Cape May. The gray afternoon sky hung low, bringing that distinct winter chill that promised the holiday season had arrived. She wrapped her hands around her mug of cinnamon tea, savoring its warmth against her palms.

"What's on your mind?" Dave asked as he entered the kitchen, his hair slightly tousled from the winter hat he'd just removed.

Margaret turned to him with a smile. "Just thinking about Christmas. It's less than two weeks away, and we still have so much to do. Especially if we're splitting our time between here and the beach house."

Dave came up behind her, wrapping his arms around her waist and resting his chin on her shoulder as they both gazed out at their property. "I picked up some fresh pine garlands yesterday. They're still in the back of the truck. Thought we could wrap them around the front porch railings here at the house. We'll need to get fresh ones for the beach house when we're ready to decorate there."

Margaret leaned back against him. "Those garlands will

look perfect on the porch. I've been picturing where to put the tree in the living room at the beach house, right by the window. And I can already imagine how festive our coastal cottage will look once we get everything decorated."

Dave smiled. "I can't wait to see it all come together." He glanced out the window at the woods behind their property. "I was thinking we could go for a walk around the property. Might clear our heads before we dive into more Christmas planning."

Margaret nodded, setting her mug down on the counter. "That sounds perfect. Let me grab my coat."

Twenty minutes later, they were walking hand in hand across their land, breath forming small clouds in the crisp air. Margaret had wrapped herself in her favorite red wool coat and a cream-colored scarf, while Dave wore his navy jacket and a knit hat.

Their farmhouse sat on many acres of land with diverse features - gardens, a greenhouse, a miniature lighthouse, a lake, and natural areas that Dave and Margaret had lovingly cultivated over the years. While they had developed much of the property, the wooded section at the back remained largely untouched, a source of constant fascination for Abby and Harper during warmer months.

"I was thinking," Margaret said as they followed a narrow path through bare oak and maple trees, "about the girls' Christmas lists. Harper's been hinting about that art set for weeks now."

Dave nodded, ducking under a low-hanging branch. "And Abby's still talking about that telescope. I found one online that's perfect for beginners."

They continued walking, their footsteps crunching on the fallen leaves and twigs. The woods around them were quiet, save for the distant call of a cardinal and the rustling of branches in the light breeze.

"I don't think we've ever walked this far northwest before,"

Dave said, glancing back the way they'd come. "We usually head toward the creek on the east side."

"Do you think we've gone too far?" Margaret asked after they had been walking for about fifteen minutes. "We should probably turn back soon if we want to—"

She stopped mid-sentence, her eyes widening as they emerged from the dense woods into a clearing. Before them stood dozens of majestic evergreens, blue spruces and pines that must have been decades old, their heights reaching thirty to forty feet into the sky.

"Dave," she whispered, squeezing his hand. "Look at these trees. They're magnificent."

Dave stood beside her, equally amazed. "From a distance, I always thought these were just part of the natural forest. I never realized they were planted in such perfect rows."

They stepped forward into what appeared to be a section of old-growth evergreens. The trees were spaced with surprising regularity, creating natural corridors between them.

"It's strange," Margaret said, turning in a slow circle to take it all in. "They seem almost... deliberately planted. But they're so old."

Dave shook his head in wonder. "Maybe part of a conservation effort? Or some long-forgotten project?"

They walked deeper among the towering trees, the scent of pine growing stronger with each step. After another few minutes of exploration, the landscape began to change. Beyond a slight rise in the terrain, they spotted something unexpected.

"Dave, look," Margaret said, pointing ahead. "Those trees are different."

As they crested the small hill, a new vista opened before them. Row upon row of smaller evergreens stretched into the distance, perfectly spaced and shaped, ranging from three to eight feet tall.

"It's a Christmas tree farm," Dave said in astonishment. "We just walked onto a Christmas tree farm."

Margaret's jaw dropped. "How have we never known about this? It's practically in our backyard."

But the farm didn't look abandoned. Though they saw no people or equipment, the trees were clearly well-maintained, with paths between rows cleared of debris and the trees themselves shaped with care. Some sections contained smaller trees, clearly ready for harvesting this season, while others held specimens that must have been growing undisturbed for decades.

"Look at these," Margaret said, approaching a row of impressive Norway spruces that must have been at least forty feet tall. "They're stunning. It's almost like they've been allowed to grow wild; no one has cut them down for Christmas trees."

Dave stepped closer to examine the ancient trees. "You're right - they're incredible. Look at the size of them." He then moved to a nearby white pine, running his hand along its branch, the needles soft against his palm. "The scent is amazing."

Margaret closed her eyes and inhaled deeply. The air was filled with the sharp, clean fragrance of pine and spruce, mingled with something else—a hint of woodsmoke, as if someone nearby was burning leaves or had a fire going in a hearth.

"Do you smell that? Like a fireplace?" she asked, opening her eyes.

Dave nodded. "Maybe there's a cabin or farmhouse on the property? Let's explore a bit more."

They walked deeper into the tree farm, marveling at the variety. Beyond the blue spruces, Douglas firs, and white pines were Fraser firs with their soft, flat needles showing silvery undersides, and even some rare varieties Margaret couldn't immediately identify.

"This place is endless," she said after they had been walking for some time. "And look at how the trees are arranged—almost like they're grouped by family gatherings. See how those tall ones seem to be protecting the smaller ones?"

Dave smiled at her observation. "You always see the poetry in things."

They continued their exploration, occasionally stopping to admire a particularly beautiful specimen or to debate whether it would fit in their living room. The gentle breeze had calmed, creating a cozy, insulated feeling, as if they were walking through an enchanted forest.

"Dave, look at this one," Margaret called, stopping beside a perfectly shaped Fraser fir about seven feet tall. "It's exactly what we've been looking for."

Dave joined her, circling the tree with an appraising eye. "You're right. It's perfect. But we can't just take it—we need to find the owner, figure out if this place is even open for business."

Margaret bit her lip, looking around the seemingly deserted farm. "I don't see any signs or buildings. Should we keep walking?"

Dave checked his watch. "We've got a little more time. Let's head in that direction—I think I see a clearing up ahead."

They made their way toward what appeared to be a break in the trees, the path widening slightly. As they walked, Margaret noticed details she had missed before—small red ribbons tied to certain trees, presumably marking them as ready for sale, and occasionally, larger trees with metal tags affixed to their trunks.

"Someone is definitely maintaining this place," she said, pointing to a freshly cut stump where a tree had recently been harvested.

The clearing they had spotted turned out to be a small meadow within the farm, surrounded on all sides by trees of varying heights. In the center stood a massive blue spruce, easily sixty feet tall and adorned with what looked like hundreds of pinecones, their scales opened wide as if ready to release their seeds.

"It's like a sentinel," Margaret said softly, gazing up at the magnificent specimen. "Standing guard over the whole farm for decades."

Dave stood beside her, equally awestruck. "I've never seen anything like it."

They stood in silence for a moment, taking in the beauty of the scene. The smell of woodsmoke was stronger here, but they still saw no sign of a cabin or house.

"We should probably head back," Dave said reluctantly, glancing at his watch again. "The girls will be home soon, and it's starting to get darker."

Margaret nodded, though she was reluctant to leave. "I can't believe we've lived next door to this for years and never knew what it really was."

As they turned to retrace their steps, Margaret noticed a small wooden sign partially covered by pine needles near the base of the massive spruce. Kneeling down, she brushed away the debris to reveal faded lettering.

"Wilson Family Christmas Trees," she read aloud. "Dave, look at this."

Dave crouched beside her, studying the weathered sign. "Wilson? I wonder if they're still around. The sign looks pretty old."

"I think we need to find out who the Wilsons are," Margaret said as Dave helped her to her feet. "Maybe we could get our tree here."

They made their way back through the rows of trees, Margaret's mind filled with questions about the mysterious Christmas tree farm that had been hiding just beyond their property line all this time.

The air grew cooler as they walked, and the scent of woodsmoke faded as they neared the edge of the tree farm. By the time they reached the boundary of their own property, the afternoon light was beginning to soften.

"We'll come back tomorrow," Dave promised as they hurried toward the warmth of their farmhouse, visible now through the bare trees. "I want to explore more of this place."

Margaret nodded, her cheeks flushed from the cold and excitement. "Me too. I bet there's more to discover beyond that clearing."

As they reached their back door, the warm golden light from the kitchen windows beckoning them inside, Margaret paused and looked back toward the woods and the hidden Christmas tree farm beyond.

"Dave," she said softly, "do you think this is the beginning of another adventure for us?"

Dave smiled, brushing a leaf from her hair. "I hope so. There's something special about this time of year—it makes even the most ordinary things seem magical."

CHAPTER TWO

The following morning, Margaret stood in the kitchen, removing a tray of ginger cookies from the oven. The spicy aroma filled the house, adding to the holiday scents that had been gradually accumulating since December began. Through the kitchen window, she could see thin wisps of chimney smoke from neighboring houses rising straight up in the still, cold air.

"Do you think we'll find the owner today?" she asked as Dave entered the kitchen, zipping up his fleece jacket.

"Hard to say," Dave replied, eyeing the cookies with interest. "But that woodsmoke we picked up yesterday means someone's out there. And the farm is clearly being maintained."

Margaret nodded, using a spatula to carefully transfer the hot cookies to a cooling rack. "I checked online last night after the girls went to bed. There's no listing for Wilson Family Christmas Trees anywhere near Cape May, at least not that I could find."

"Weird," Dave said, picking up a cookie from the rack and taking a bite despite the heat. He closed his eyes for a moment, savoring the spicy sweetness. "These are perfect. Nothing beats a cookie fresh from the oven."

Margaret smiled at his enjoyment. "Careful, you'll burn your tongue."

Dave chuckled. "Fair enough. Ready to head out once you're done here?"

Margaret looked at the remaining cookie dough in the bowl. "Let me just wrap this up. I'll bake the rest when we get back."

She quickly covered the bowl with plastic wrap and placed it in the refrigerator. "All set. Let's go."

They stepped outside into the crisp morning air and followed the same path as the day before, walking in comfortable silence through the woods at the back of their property. The fallen leaves crunched beneath their boots, and birdsong occasionally punctuated the quiet.

"It's this way," Dave said when they reached the point where the dense woods gave way to the towering evergreens. "I've been thinking about this place all night."

"Me too," Margaret admitted. "I had dreams about endless rows of Christmas trees."

As they entered the Christmas tree farm, the scent of pine enveloped them once again. They walked past the first section of massive, decades-old trees and into the area with the smaller, carefully shaped trees ready for harvesting.

"Let's try a different direction today," Dave suggested, pointing to the west. "We explored mostly north and east yesterday."

Margaret agreed, and they veered onto a path that wound between rows of Fraser firs and blue spruces. After walking for about ten minutes, the path curved around a dense thicket of holly bushes, their bright-red berries vivid against the dark-green leaves.

"Dave," Margaret said suddenly, stopping in her tracks. "Look over there."

In the distance, perhaps a quarter mile away, a thin column of smoke rose lazily into the blue sky. As they moved forward, a small cabin came into view, nestled among a cluster of tall pines. It was a simple structure, built of weathered logs with a metal roof that gleamed in the sunlight. A covered porch wrapped around the front, and a stone chimney rose from the far end.

"That must be where the woodsmoke was coming from yesterday," Dave said, his pace quickening with excitement.

As they drew closer, details emerged—window boxes still holding the dried remnants of summer flowers, a neat stack of firewood along one side of the cabin, and a few rocking chairs on the porch. In one of those chairs sat a figure, barely visible from their vantage point.

Margaret felt a flutter of nervous anticipation. "Do you think that's Mr. Wilson?"

"One way to find out," Dave replied, guiding them toward a path that led directly to the cabin.

They had covered about half the distance when the figure in the rocking chair seemed to notice them. He stood up—it was definitely a man, they could see now—and moved to the edge of the porch, one hand shading his eyes against the sun as he peered in their direction.

"Hello there!" the man called out, his voice carrying clearly across the distance.

Margaret and Dave waved and continued forward. As they approached, they could see that the man was older, perhaps in his seventies, with a full head of silver hair and a neatly trimmed beard to match. He wore a red-and-black flannel shirt over a thermal henley, jeans, and well-worn work boots. His face was weathered but kind, with laugh lines etched deeply around his eyes.

"Welcome, welcome," he said as they reached the edge of his yard. A simple split-rail fence marked the boundary, with a gate that stood open. "Don't often get visitors this time of year, except folks coming for trees, of course."

"Hello," Margaret said warmly. "I'm Margaret, and this is

my husband, Dave. We discovered your Christmas tree farm yesterday, and we were hoping to meet the owner."

The man's face lit up with a broad smile. "Well, you've found him. Tom Wilson, at your service." He extended a hand first to Dave, then to Margaret. His grip was firm despite his age, his skin rough from years of outdoor work.

"It's a pleasure to meet you, Tom," Dave said. "We actually live just beyond the eastern edge of your property. We've been there for years but only discovered the tree farm yesterday."

Tom's bushy eyebrows rose in surprise. "You don't say! You must be the folks who bought the old Meyer place, then?"

Margaret nodded. "That's us. We've been there for a few years now."

Tom shook his head in wonder. "Well, I'll be. Neighbors all this time and never crossed paths. But then, I don't get out to the eastern edge much these days." He gestured toward the porch. "Why don't you join me up here? It's a nice spot to enjoy the afternoon."

They followed him up the three wooden steps to the porch, where several rocking chairs were arranged in a conversational grouping. A small table stood nearby with a mug of what looked like coffee.

"Can I offer you some coffee?" Tom asked. "Just made a fresh pot."

"That's very kind, thank you," Margaret said. "Coffee would be lovely."

"I'll take a cup too," Dave added.

"Coming right up," Tom said, disappearing into the cabin. He returned moments later with three mugs of steaming coffee and set them on the small table. "Milk or sugar?"

"Black is fine for me," Dave said.

"Just a splash of milk if you have it," Margaret replied.

Tom nodded and went back inside, returning with a small pitcher of milk. Once they were all settled in the rocking chairs with their coffee, Tom took a sip and sighed contentedly.

"Your farm is absolutely beautiful," Margaret said, cradling her mug in both hands. "We were amazed when we stumbled upon it yesterday."

Tom nodded, a wistful expression crossing his face. "Been my life's work, this place. My father started it back in 1942, and I took over when he passed in 1970. That's over fifty years now I've been tending these trees." He gestured toward the vast expanse of evergreens spreading out before them. "Every one of 'em planted by either me or my father. Some of those oldest ones, the real giants, those were among his first plantings."

"The blue spruce in the clearing," Dave said. "The really massive one. That must be one of the originals?"

"Good eye," Tom replied with a nod. "That's the very first tree my father planted here. It marked the beginning of everything. He planted it right after he bought the land in '42." He smiled at the memory. "He always said that tree was special, that it represented the future of this place."

"How many acres is the farm?" Dave asked, taking a sip of his coffee.

"Twenty-eight, all told," Tom said. "Started with just five when my father bought it, but he added parcels over the years, and I picked up the last ten acres in the '80s. Wanted to make sure we had room to rotate the plantings properly." His voice took on a note of pride. "Never had to clear-cut any section. Always planted in phases so there'd be trees of all ages growing together. More natural that way."

Margaret leaned forward, genuinely interested. "How many trees do you sell each season?"

Tom thought for a moment. "Oh, varies year to year. Used to be upwards of five hundred when I was younger and could handle the work. These days, it's more like a hundred, hundred and fifty. Mostly to families who've been coming here for generations." His expression grew a shade more serious. "That's one of the hardest parts about the decision I've had to make."

"What decision is that?" Dave asked.

Tom sighed, setting his mug down on the table. "I've been thinking about selling the farm. At seventy-six, it's getting harder to keep up with it all. My knees aren't what they used to be." He looked out at the rows of trees with a wistful expression. "But I'm just exploring my options at this point. Nothing definite yet."

Margaret nodded sympathetically. "It must be difficult to consider parting with a place that means so much to you."

"It is," Tom agreed. "This place has been my whole life." He picked up his mug again. "A realtor friend of mine suggested I consider listing it, just to see what kind of interest there might be."

"Have you had any interest?" Dave asked.

A troubled expression crossed Tom's face. "That's the thing. A development company came sniffing around. They're interested in the property for a subdivision." He gestured toward the tree farm. "Can you imagine? All this, turned into streets and cookie-cutter houses." He shook his head. "I know progress is progress, but it doesn't sit right with me, somehow."

Margaret glanced at Dave, a silent communication passing between them. "But you haven't made any decisions yet?" she asked.

"No, not at all," Tom replied. "I'm still weighing my options. Part of me isn't even sure I want to sell." He chuckled ruefully. "At my age, you'd think I wouldn't be such a sentimentalist."

Dave leaned forward in his chair. "How long has the farm been providing trees to Cape May families?"

Tom's face brightened at the question. "Oh, since 1945. My father started selling trees soon after he established the farm. Said he wanted to be part of bringing joy to families during the holidays." He took a sip of his coffee. "First year, he sold maybe twenty trees, all to neighbors and friends. By the

'50s, word had spread, and families would make a day of it, coming out to choose their tree."

"That's wonderful," Margaret said. "So much history here."

Tom nodded. "Used to have hayrides for the kids back in the '70s and '80s. My wife, Nanette, she'd make hot cider and her famous snickerdoodles. We'd have a bonfire on the weekends, and people would stay well past dark, singing carols and telling stories." His eyes grew distant with the memories. "Those were good days."

"Is your wife still involved with the farm?" Margaret asked.

Tom chuckled. "Oh yes, Nanette's still very much the heart of this place. She's just out running errands in town today. Probably picking up more baking supplies—she's been making her famous apple cinnamon bread for the tree customers." His face softened. "Fifty-three years together, and she still surprises me. Got more energy than I do these days, that's for sure."

"She sounds wonderful," Margaret said.

"That she is," Tom agreed with a fond smile. "Toughest and kindest person I ever knew. You'll have to meet her next time you come by."

They sat in companionable silence for a moment, each lost in their own thoughts as they rocked gently in their chairs. The sun was climbing higher in the sky, casting long shadows across the tree farm.

"Would you mind if we walked around a bit more?" Dave asked eventually. "We'd love to see more of the farm if that's alright."

"Of course, of course," Tom said, rising from his chair with a slight grimace that suggested his knees were indeed troubling him. "Let me give you the tour. Not the full tour, mind you—that would take all day—but I can show you some of my favorite spots."

As they prepared to leave the porch, Margaret noticed a framed photograph visible through the front window. It showed a much younger Tom with a beautiful dark-haired woman—presumably Nanette—standing in front of the blue spruce, though it was considerably smaller than it was now. They were flanked by two children, a boy and a girl, both with their mother's dark hair and their father's bright-blue eyes.

"Is that your family?" she asked.

Tom paused to look at the photograph through the window, his expression softening. "Yes, that's us. 1985, I believe. Sarah was twelve, and Tommy Jr. was ten." His gaze lingered on the image. "Hard to believe that was forty years ago."

He shook himself from his reverie and gestured toward the path. "Come on, then. We've got plenty of morning left, and there's much to see."

As they followed Tom down the porch steps, Margaret couldn't help but think about the developer's offer and what it would mean for this beautiful, historic farm. The thought of all these magnificent trees being cut down to make way for a subdivision filled her with an unexpected sense of loss.

She caught Dave's eye, and she could tell he was thinking the same thing. But for now, they simply followed Tom along the path as he began to tell them about the different varieties of trees and the stories behind them, his voice animated with the passion of a man sharing his life's work.

Liz stepped back to admire the reclaimed wood shelving she'd just finished installing against the exposed brick wall of Furnish & Feast. She pulled her cardigan tighter around herself as she surveyed what would soon display her carefully restored furniture pieces. After weeks of working late into the night and through weekends, the exhaustion was setting in, but seeing the space take shape made it worthwhile.

"What do you think?" she asked, turning to Greg, who was measuring the counter space on the opposite side of the room.

Greg looked up from his tape measure and smiled. "It's perfect. The wood tones really pop against the brick."

The transformation of the former Heirloom restaurant was well underway. After six weeks of intensive renovations, they had made significant progress, though much work remained before their opening. The space had been divided into two distinct but harmonious sections. On one side, Liz was creating an elegant showroom for her furniture restorations. On the other, Greg had designed a streamlined lunch counter with an open prep area behind it.

"I can't believe how much we've accomplished already," Liz said, running her hand along the smooth surface of the shelving. "This space is really starting to take shape."

Greg set down his measuring tape and crossed the room to stand beside her. "It feels right, doesn't it? Like this is what the space was always meant to be."

Liz nodded, leaning into him as he wrapped an arm around her shoulders. The journey to this point hadn't been easy. There had been permit delays, contractor issues, and budget concerns. But standing here now, seeing their vision taking shape, made all the challenges worthwhile.

"The deliveries today will help us plan the next phase," Greg said. "Having the actual furniture in the space will make it easier to visualize how everything should come together."

The sound of a truck engine rumbling outside interrupted him. They exchanged excited glances and hurried to the front window.

"Perfect timing," Greg said as a large delivery truck pulled up in front of the shop. "That must be the café furniture."

They stepped outside as the delivery driver jumped down from the cab and slid open the truck's rear door.

"Delivery for Furnish and Feast?" the driver asked, clipboard in hand.

"That's us," Greg confirmed, signing the offered form.

"Great. Got six pallets for you. Where do you want 'em?"

Greg pointed to the side door. "Through here inside would be perfect. We can take it from here."

As Greg and Liz followed the driver inside, they were eager to see the café tables and chairs they'd carefully selected from a restaurant supply catalog. They had chosen a set of rustic wooden tables with sleek metal chairs—a perfect complement to the aesthetic they'd created.

The driver began unloading with a hand truck, positioning the first pallet in the center of Greg's side of the space. "I'll grab the rest," he said, heading back to the truck.

Liz approached the shrink-wrapped pallet, peering at its contents. "Something looks off," she said, frowning slightly. "These boxes seem way too small for café tables and chairs."

Greg grabbed a box cutter from the counter and sliced through the plastic wrap. As the covering fell away, they both stared in confusion.

"Are those... children's tables?" Liz asked, reaching for one of the small round tables.

Greg picked up what appeared to be a chair and set it on the floor. It stood approximately eighteen inches high, with a bright-yellow plastic seat and metal legs.

"This can't be right," he said, looking at the packing slip attached to the pallet. "This is addressed to us, but this definitely isn't what we ordered."

The delivery driver returned with another pallet, also shrink-wrapped and similarly sized.

"There's been a mistake," Greg explained to the driver. "This is children's furniture. We ordered café tables and chairs."

The driver shrugged. "I just deliver what's on the truck, sir. You'll have to take it up with the supplier." He continued with his deliveries and left once all the pallets were unloaded.

Greg pulled out his phone and began scrolling through his emails for the supplier's contact information while the driver continued unloading. By the time all six pallets were inside, they were surrounded by what appeared to be a complete preschool classroom set—tiny tables, miniature chairs, colorful cubbies, and even a small reading nook with cushions shaped like animals.

"This is absurd," Liz said, watching as Greg attempted to sit at one of the tables. His knees were practically at chest level, the tiny chair creaking ominously beneath him.

"Not exactly the casual lunch counter we were planning," Greg remarked, his voice strained as he tried to fit his adult frame into the child-sized furniture.

Liz couldn't help but laugh at the sight of her husband hunched over the tiny table, looking like an adult who had wandered into a kindergarten classroom.

"Don't laugh," Greg protested, though he was fighting back his own smile. "This is a disaster."

"I know, I know," Liz said, composing herself. "Can you reach the supplier?"

Greg carefully extricated himself from the miniature chair. "Let me try calling them." He dialed the supplier's number he'd found earlier. After a moment, his expression soured. "Great. I'm on hold. Apparently, their customer service department is experiencing 'higher than normal call volume.'"

Liz was about to respond when the bell above the door jingled, signaling another arrival.

"Excuse me," called a voice from the entrance. "I have a delivery for Furnish and Feast?"

A different delivery driver stood in the doorway, clipboard in hand. "Got eight boxes for you. Home décor items, it says here."

"At least something's going right," Liz muttered, going to sign for the packages. "You can bring them over here."

While Greg continued to wait on hold, Liz directed the second driver to place the boxes near her display shelves. These were the carefully curated decorative items she'd ordered to complement her furniture pieces—silk flowers, tasteful vases, picture frames, throw pillows, ribbons, and seasonal accessories that customers could purchase alongside the larger furniture items.

As the driver left, Liz eagerly opened the first box, pulling away the packing material to reveal... a hot-pink feather boa?

"What on earth?" she murmured, reaching deeper into the box.

Her fingers closed around something plastic, and she pulled out a headband adorned with miniature plastic hunks in cowboy hats bobbing on springs.

"Oh my goodness," she exclaimed, pulling out another feather boa and a sparkly tiara with attached veil. "This is definitely not what I ordered."

Greg looked over, momentarily distracted from his phone call. "What did you get?"

Liz rifled through the box then started laughing. "Bachelorette party supplies, from the looks of it." She held up a hot-pink sash that read "Bride-to-Be" in silver sequins.

Greg abandoned his futile hold music and joined Liz as she opened another box. This one contained an assortment of novelty shot glasses with cheeky sayings, drinking straws with tiny firefighters sliding down poles, colorful drink umbrellas, and a banner that proclaimed "From Miss to Mrs" in glittery letters.

"Well, this is unexpected," Liz said with an amused smile as she examined some chocolate molds shaped like muscular torsos.

Greg picked up the packing slip attached to the box. "It's addressed to 'Bridesmaids & Beaus' in Atlantic City. Looks like some kind of bachelorette party supply store." He looked around at the pallets of children's furniture. "And I'm guessing our café furniture is sitting in a preschool somewhere."

Liz sank down onto a nearby stepladder. "This can't be happening," she said with a sigh. "What are we supposed to do with all this?"

Greg returned to his phone, which was still playing bland jazz hold music. After another minute, he finally reached a customer service representative. Liz watched as his expression shifted from hopeful to concerned to outright dismayed.

"What do you mean closed for the holiday?" he asked incredulously. "It's December 15th... No, I understand company policy, but this is an emergency... Yes, I realize you're just the call center... No, I don't want to leave a message..."

By the time Greg ended the call, Liz had opened all eight boxes of bachelorette party supplies and arranged them in a comical display on one of her antique tables—feather boas in every color of the rainbow, tiaras with mini veils attached, novelty sunglasses, sparkly "Bride Squad" sashes, and enough glitter to decorate a small parade float. The elegant antique table was now transformed into what looked like the aftermath of a bridal shop explosion.

"Well?" she asked as Greg approached.

"The supplier is closed for their annual holiday break until January 3rd," he said, running a hand through his hair. "The customer service rep couldn't help beyond logging our complaint for when they reopen."

"January 3rd?" Liz repeated incredulously. "That's weeks away!"

"It gets worse," Greg continued. "Even if we could somehow return these items now, they wouldn't be able to ship our correct orders until after they reopen. We're looking at mid-January at the earliest."

Liz stared at the collection of party favors on her lovingly restored Victorian table, then at the miniature furniture scattered throughout Greg's lunch area. The juxtaposition was so absurd that she felt a bubble of hysterical laughter rising in her throat.

"So we're stuck with a preschool café and a bachelorette party supply store?" she asked, her voice quavering.

Greg nodded solemnly then suddenly burst out laughing.

"Can you imagine? 'Welcome to Furnish & Feast, where the chairs are tiny and the décor is totally cheeky!'"

Liz tried to maintain her composure, but the image Greg painted was too ridiculous. A giggle escaped her, then another, until she was laughing so hard tears streamed down her face.

"What are we going to do?" she gasped between fits of laughter.

Greg wiped his eyes, still chuckling. "I have no idea. Return everything when the supplier reopens, I guess?"

"I suppose we'll have to," Liz agreed, her laughter gradually subsiding. But the smile remained on her face as she looked around at the absurd collection of items surrounding them. The mix-up was ridiculous, yes, but somehow it had broken the tension of the past few weeks. She met Greg's eyes, her expression both amused and thoughtful. In that shared glance, they both acknowledged how utterly exhausted they'd become—the dark circles under their eyes, the constant muscle aches, the way they'd been pushing themselves to the breaking point with long days. Neither had wanted to be the first to suggest slowing down, but their bodies were clearly demanding rest.

CHAPTER THREE

Dale arrived at Donna's Restaurant just after eight in the morning. He unlocked the front door, flipped on the lights, and made his way through the dining room toward the kitchen. He set his bag down on the counter and began pulling out containers of ingredients he'd prepped the night before.

Today was important. He needed to finalize the holiday specials menu, and Dale had been experimenting with several new ideas that he was eager for Donna to try. The holiday season was crucial for the restaurant's bottom line, helping to sustain him through the lean months that followed. Donna had stepped in to help manage the increased holiday business. This year, he was determined to create something memorable that would keep tables filled even on weeknights.

The back door opened as Dale was setting up his ingredients, and Donna walked in, carrying a small cardboard box.

"Morning," she called cheerfully. She set the box on the counter and began unpacking various bottles. "I picked up the spirits we talked about for the cocktail testing."

Dale leaned over and kissed her cheek. "Perfect timing. I'm just getting started on the cranberry sage reduction."

"The aroma is already amazing," Donna said, arranging the bottles in a neat row. "I'm excited to try it."

"The sage is the key," Dale said, pouring fresh cranberries into a saucepan. "The earthiness will balance the sweetness of the cranberries. It'll be perfect for the turkey special."

Donna nodded and continued unpacking her supplies. "By the way, did you order those ceramic serving platters we talked about? They'll give the holiday specials a more elegant presentation."

"Already done," Dale confirmed, stirring his reduction. "They should arrive tomorrow."

They worked in comfortable silence for a while, Dale focusing on his reduction while Donna began experimenting with the spirits she'd brought. The kitchen filled with warm, inviting aromas—the tart sweetness of simmering cranberries and earthy sage from Dale's reduction mingling with cinnamon, cloves, and allspice as they both developed potential recipes for their winter offerings.

"Try this," Donna said eventually, holding out a small cup with an amber liquid. "I'm thinking of calling it 'Winter Sunrise.' Bourbon base with cinnamon-orange syrup and a hint of cardamom."

Dale sipped it and nodded appreciatively. "That's good. Really good. But maybe a touch more cardamom? It gets lost under the orange."

Donna made a note on her clipboard. "I'll adjust the ratio. What about the cranberry sage reduction? Is it ready yet?"

Dale stirred the simmering mixture then lifted the spoon, watching as the thickened reduction coated it evenly. "Almost there. Give it another five minutes."

Suddenly, a booming bass line cut through the quiet kitchen, startling them both. The music was so loud that Dale could feel it vibrating through the floor.

"What is that?" he asked, looking toward the front of the restaurant.

Donna frowned and set down her spoon. "No idea."

Dale wiped his hands on a towel and walked through the dining room to the front windows. Donna followed close behind. Outside, in the parking lot adjacent to the restaurant, a flurry of activity was taking place. Workers in neon-yellow vests were unloading equipment from several trucks, setting up what appeared to be carnival rides. A massive speaker system was being positioned near the property line, currently blasting "Jingle Bell Rock" at a volume that seemed excessive even for daytime, let alone early morning.

"Is that a Ferris wheel?" Donna asked, squinting at the half-assembled structure rising from the center of the parking lot.

Dale pressed his face closer to the glass. "Looks like it. And I think that's a carousel over there. What is all this? And how did it just appear like that? It wasn't here when I arrived."

Without waiting for an answer, he pushed open the front door and stepped outside. Donna followed close behind. They approached a worker who was unraveling extension cords from a large spool.

"Excuse me," Dale called over the music. "What's going on here?"

The worker looked up, seemingly surprised to see them. "Setting up for the Christmas carnival. It starts tomorrow night."

"Christmas carnival?" Donna repeated. "We weren't notified about any carnival."

The worker shrugged. "City approved it last month. It's running every night from 4 PM to 11 PM until December 23rd. Rides, games, food stands, the works. Should be a big draw."

Dale felt his stomach tighten. "And the music will be this loud the entire time?"

"Oh, this is just testing the system," the worker said casually. "But yeah, there'll be Christmas music playing throughout the event. Can't have a Christmas carnival without the tunes, right? The volume'll be cranked up even more when it's running."

He turned back to his work, effectively ending the conversation. Dale and Donna exchanged worried glances and walked back toward the restaurant, the music still pounding behind them.

"This is going to be a disaster," Dale said once they were back inside, though the music was still clearly audible despite the closed doors and windows. "Our dinner service starts at five. How are people supposed to enjoy a meal with that racket going on?"

Donna leaned against the hostess stand, her brow furrowed. "And where are our customers supposed to park? That carnival is taking up at least half of the shared lot."

Dale ran a hand through his hair. "Parking is already tight in this part of Cape May, and now this."

"We couldn't have known this would happen," Donna reasoned, though she sounded worried. "But we need to figure out what to do. We can't afford to lose our holiday customers."

They returned to the kitchen, where the cranberry sage reduction was now bubbling over the edge of the pot. Dale rushed to turn down the heat, salvaging what he could of the mixture.

"Perfect metaphor for our situation," he said bitterly, stirring the reduced concoction. "Everything boiling over at once."

Donna tasted one of her cocktail experiments, then grimaced and set it aside. "We could try to see if there's anything that can be done about the noise levels at least."

"I'm not sure how much can be changed at this point," Dale said, tasting the mixture. "It seems like everything's already been approved and is moving forward."

"Then maybe we should try to adapt somehow," Donna suggested, leaning against the counter. "We might be able to find some way to make this work in our favor."

Dale considered this as he spooned some of the cranberry

reduction over a small piece of turkey. "That's thinking outside the box, but I don't know. Our whole concept is built around quality food and craft cocktails. Not..." He gestured vaguely in the direction of the blaring music.

"Well, we have to do something," Donna insisted. "We can't just hide in here and hope for the best."

Dale handed her the plate with the turkey sample. "Try this first, then we'll figure out our carnival strategy."

Donna took a bite, and her eyes widened. "Okay, that's even better than I expected. This is going to be a hit."

"Perfect," Dale said with a small smile, though his mind was still on the carnival outside. "At least something's going right today."

They spent the next hour finishing their taste tests, though their concentration was repeatedly broken by the music and occasional mechanical noises from the carnival setup. By nine-thirty, they had finalized most of their holiday menu items, but the question of how to deal with their new neighbor remained unresolved.

"Let's go take another look," Donna suggested as they cleaned up the kitchen. "Maybe it won't be as bad as we think."

They walked back to the front of the restaurant and stepped outside again. The carnival setup had progressed significantly in the past two hours. The Ferris wheel was now fully assembled, towering over the surrounding buildings. Food stands lined the perimeter of the parking lot, and workers were stringing colorful lights between poles. The music had, mercifully, been turned down, though Dale suspected this was temporary.

A man in jeans, holding a walkie talkie, was now directing the workers. He noticed Dale and Donna watching and approached them with a practiced smile.

"Good morning! I'm Chase, event coordinator for Winter Wonderland Enterprises. You must be the owners of this lovely establishment?"

Dale nodded stiffly. "Dale and Donna. We own Donna's Restaurant."

"Wonderful to meet you both," Chase said, extending his hand, which Dale reluctantly shook. "I hope our setup isn't causing too much disturbance. We're trying to get the noisiest parts done early."

"Your crew works fast," Dale observed, looking at the progress they'd made in just a short time. "None of this was here when I arrived this morning."

Chase beamed with pride. "That's our specialty! We have a system—the entire carnival can be set up in under four hours. We call ourselves the 'pop-up pros.' We've refined our process over years of doing this. Our team comes in waves—first the marking crew, then the foundation team, followed by the rides crew and finally the finishing team."

"Actually, we're concerned about how this carnival will impact our business," Donna said directly. "The music this morning was extremely loud, and you've taken a significant portion of the parking that our customers use."

Chase's smile dimmed slightly. "I understand your concerns, but I can assure you that the Winter Wonderland Christmas Carnival will benefit all local businesses. We're expecting to draw hundreds of visitors each night, many of whom will be looking for a nice dinner before or after their carnival experience."

"If they can find parking," Dale muttered.

Chase cleared his throat. "We've arranged with the city for additional street parking to be made available during the event. And as for the music, we'll ensure the speakers are directed away from your establishment during peak dining hours."

Dale wasn't convinced, but before he could respond, a worker called Chase over to address some issue with the carousel.

"Excuse me," Chase said, already backing away. "Feel free

to stop by for the grand opening. We'd love to have you experience the magic of the carnival firsthand!"

As he hurried away, Dale turned to Donna. "Did you believe a word of that?"

Donna sighed. "Not really. But I'm trying to stay positive. Maybe he's right about one thing—it could bring more people to the area who might decide to eat with us."

They watched as workers began testing the Ferris wheel, the massive structure slowly rotating against the brightening morning sky. The first car reached the top and paused there, offering what Dale had to admit was probably a spectacular view of Cape May.

"So what do we do?" he asked, watching the Ferris wheel turn.

Donna slipped her hand into his. "I don't think we have much choice but to adapt. We can't move the restaurant, so we either work with this situation or let it work against us."

Dale squeezed her hand, his eyes still on the turning Ferris wheel. "I guess we'll find out soon enough what kind of impact this will have."

As they stood there, another Christmas song began playing through the speakers, the volume creeping up once again. The carnival was coming, whether they liked it or not, and their holiday season had just become a lot more complicated than a cranberry sage reduction.

Judy adjusted her shawl around her shoulders as she and Bob settled into their corner table at Charlotte's Way Inn, a charming historic establishment. The dining room had been transformed for the holidays with subtle elegance: white string lights draped along exposed wooden beams, small potted poinsettias on each table, and sprigs of holly tucked into polished brass sconces on the walls. The soft lighting cast a warm glow over the intimate space, and the background music of instrumental Christmas classics played at just the right volume for conversation.

"This was a good choice," Judy said, looking around appreciatively. "Not too crowded for a weeknight."

Bob nodded as he studied the menu.

"The scallop dish looks wonderful," Judy said, slipping on her reading glasses to examine her menu.

After they placed their orders, Bob reached across the table and took Judy's hand. They talked quietly while they waited, and continued their conversation as they enjoyed their meal—calamari and French onion soup to start, followed by scallops for Judy and filet mignon for Bob.

They were halfway through their main courses when there was a sudden scraping sound from the far corner of the restaurant. They both looked up to see two staff members moving a small table to make room for what appeared to be a karaoke machine being wheeled in by a third employee.

"What's going on?" Bob asked, looking curious.

Before Judy could respond, the hostess stepped into the center of the dining room and cleared her throat.

"Good evening, everyone! As advertised, tonight is our first ever Christmas Karaoke Night at Charlotte's Way Inn!" She gestured toward the machine, which was now being plugged in. "We'll be starting in about ten minutes, so finish up those delicious entrees and think about what holiday classic you might want to share with us tonight!"

Bob and Judy exchanged glances.

"Did you see anything about karaoke when you made the reservation?" Judy asked quietly.

Bob shook his head. "Not a word. Must be a new thing they're trying."

"Well," Judy said, cutting another piece of her scallop, "I suppose it could be entertaining."

By the time they finished their main courses, the karaoke setup was complete. A red-faced man in his thirties, clearly bolstered by several drinks, had just finished a painfully off-key rendition of "I Saw Mommy Kissing Santa Claus" that had Bob wincing beside her. The sparse applause that followed seemed more like relief that the performance had ended rather than appreciation.

"Should we get the check?" Bob whispered, leaning closer to Judy.

Before she could answer, the hostess was back at the microphone.

"Let's give it up again for Mike! Who's next? Come on, don't be shy!"

After an awkward pause, a young woman with long dark hair stood up from a table near the front. She approached the microphone with visible nervousness, tucking her hair behind her ear as she scrolled through the song options.

"I guess I'll try 'All I Want for Christmas Is You,'" she said softly into the microphone.

When the music started, Judy prepared herself for another uncomfortable performance, but to her surprise, the young woman's voice was lovely—clear and controlled, with just the right amount of emotional delivery. Several conversations around the restaurant died down as diners turned to listen.

When she finished, the applause was genuine, though still somewhat subdued. The young woman hurried back to her table, blushing as her friends congratulated her.

"That was actually quite good," Bob remarked, signaling to their server for the bill.

"It was," Judy agreed. "But I think I've had enough excitement for one evening."

Their server was just bringing their check when the hostess approached the microphone again.

"Anyone else feeling the Christmas spirit tonight?"

The restaurant had grown quieter, most diners focused on their meals or conversations, with little interest in participating.

Judy was reaching for her purse when movement near the bar caught her attention.

An older man—older than themselves, Judy guessed, perhaps in his mid-eighties—was making his way slowly toward the karaoke machine. He wore a navy blazer with a red pocket square, gray slacks, and a collared shirt, but his clothes hung somewhat loosely on his thin frame. His silver hair was neatly combed, though a few strands had escaped to drift across his forehead. Despite a slight stoop to his shoulders, he carried himself with dignity.

"Hold on," Judy said to Bob, who was counting out bills for the tip. "Let's see what he sings."

The man reached the microphone and smiled politely at the hostess as she helped him navigate the song selection. Most of the restaurant continued with their meals and conversations, barely acknowledging the man's presence.

"I think I'll sing 'White Christmas,'" he said into the microphone, his voice slightly wavery but pleasant. "It was my wife's favorite."

The opening notes filled the restaurant, and the man closed his eyes. When he began to sing, Judy felt a small shock of surprise. His voice was rich and resonant, with the kind of depth that comes only from years of practice. There was a slight vibrato that spoke of his years, but it only added character to the performance.

Bob paused with his wallet halfway back to his pocket. "Well, now," he said softly.

The man swayed gently with the music, one hand gripping the microphone stand, the other gesturing slightly with the melody. His eyes remained closed, a small smile playing at the corners of his mouth. Despite the quality of his performance, most diners continued their conversations, throwing only occasional glances his way.

"He's quite good," Judy whispered.

"Very," Bob agreed, settling back into his chair. "I wonder if he was a professional."

As the song neared its end, the man opened his eyes, his gaze distant, as if looking at something—or someone—only he could see. He finished with a gentle, sustained note that faded perfectly with the music.

There was a smattering of applause, slightly more enthusiastic than for the first performer but nowhere near what Judy felt the man deserved. He nodded graciously then looked back at the machine.

"If it's all right, I'd like to do one more," he said. "Have Yourself a Merry Little Christmas."

The hostess smiled and cued up the song. As the introduction played, Bob leaned forward, studying the man more closely.

"Look at his left hand," he said quietly to Judy. "Wedding ring."

Judy noticed it then—a simple gold band that looked permanently affixed to his finger after decades of wear. She thought about the man's earlier comment about his wife's favorite song and felt a pang in her heart.

This second performance was even more moving than the first. The man's voice conveyed both melancholy and hope, perfectly capturing the bittersweet nature of the song. His voice caught almost imperceptibly during one of the most poignant lines about being together through the years, but enough that Judy felt tears prickling at the corners of her eyes.

Still, the restaurant bustled around them, most patrons oblivious to the small moment of beauty unfolding in their midst. A waiter dropped silverware with a clatter. A group near the door laughed loudly at a shared joke. A child at a family table whined about being tired.

Yet the man seemed transported to another time and place, his smile genuine as he sang. His joy in the performance was evident, regardless of whether anyone was paying proper attention.

When he finished, he gave a small, almost formal bow, handed the microphone back to the hostess, and made his way slowly back to the bar, where he sat alone with what looked like a glass of soda.

"That was lovely," Judy said, dabbing at her eyes with her napkin.

Bob nodded, his expression thoughtful. "It was." He glanced at the check, then back at the man. "What do you say we order some dessert?"

Judy raised an eyebrow. "You never want dessert."

"I'm making an exception," Bob replied with a small smile. "I'd like to hear if he sings anything else."

Judy smiled. "That sounds perfect."

They ordered coffee and a slice of cheesecake to share. As they waited, the hostess tried unsuccessfully to convince other diners to participate. Eventually, the red-faced man from earlier returned for another enthusiastic but tuneless performance.

Judy watched as the older man at the bar nursed his drink, occasionally tapping his fingers on the counter in time with the background music. "I wonder what his story is," she said softly.

"A lot of life in those eyes," Bob observed. "Probably has some tales to tell."

As they finished their dessert, the hostess announced a final call for performers before karaoke would end for the evening. Judy glanced hopefully toward the bar, but the older man remained seated, seemingly content with his two performances. He sipped his drink slowly, a faint smile on his face as he watched another brave volunteer take the stage. His evening of sharing music had clearly come to a satisfying end.

CHAPTER FOUR

Margaret pushed open the door of The Book Nook, welcomed by the cheerful jingle of bells and the familiar scent of paper, coffee, and cinnamon that always seemed to permeate the cozy bookstore. Soft Christmas music played from hidden speakers, adding to the festive atmosphere. A tabletop Christmas tree sat on the counter, decorated with tiny ornaments shaped like books, while garlands of white lights draped across bookshelves bathed the space in soft illumination. The prominent holiday book display took center stage in the shop's main area, drawing immediate attention with its festive arrangement.

A few customers browsed quietly among the shelves, and Margaret could hear the whir of the espresso machine as an employee prepared a cappuccino at the counter.

"Sarah?" she called, looking around but not seeing her friend.

"Over here!" Sarah's voice came from somewhere behind the tall holiday book arrangement. "Working on restocking!"

Margaret made her way around the new releases table and found Sarah kneeling beside the Christmas display, organizing and rearranging the holiday books that had been quickly depleted by eager shoppers. Several boxes of new inventory surrounded her on the floor—holiday fiction bestsellers, beautifully illustrated classics, seasonal cooking guides, and what appeared to be at least a dozen different editions of "A Christmas Carol."

"I can't decide," Sarah said without looking up, "if I should keep organizing by genre or switch to theme. The display keeps getting ransacked every day." She sighed, placing another stack of books on a nearly empty shelf. "I'm glad they're selling, but keeping this section organized has become a daily challenge."

"When did you last take a break?" Margaret asked, bending down to pick up a beautiful edition of "The Nutcracker" that had slid from one of the piles.

Sarah glanced up, seeming to truly notice Margaret for the first time. "Oh! Hi! What time is it?"

"Almost noon."

"Already?" Sarah rubbed her eyes. "I've been at this since eight. The Christmas book event starts tomorrow, and nothing's ready."

Margaret gestured to the display. "It looks like you've made good progress."

Sarah sighed, sitting back on her heels. "This is just one small part. I still have the window display, the signing table for the local author tomorrow, and..." She paused. "I've also volunteered to host the cookie exchange."

"The annual cookie exchange?" Margaret asked, sliding a stack of books aside to make room on the floor. She sat down cross-legged across from her friend. "Isn't that usually at the community center?"

"It was supposed to be," Sarah explained. "But I got a call yesterday because a pipe burst at the community center and it won't be repaired in time. They were looking for another place, and I offered the store.

"And now I have less than a week to figure out how to accommodate thirty to forty people and all their cookies." She gestured around the store. "This will need way more space than when I hosted Blake Terry's book signing. I'll need tables for all the cookie displays, serving areas, and space for people to mingle. Not to mention, there's the possibility of crumbs and sticky fingers around my books."

"When is it scheduled for?"

"December 22nd." Sarah pushed herself to her feet. "Let me grab some fresh coffee, and I'll give you the full picture of my madness."

Margaret followed Sarah to the checkout counter, where the coffee equipment was set up at one end. As Sarah poured them each a cup from the freshly brewed pot, Margaret noticed how busy her friend seemed with all the holiday preparations.

"You know," Margaret said, "it's okay to say no sometimes, even to good causes."

Sarah handed her a steaming mug. "I get it. But I thought it would be a nice thing to do. Plus, having some extra people in the store might boost holiday sales."

Margaret nodded, taking a sip of her coffee. "Well, you're not doing this alone. I'll help you organize it."

Sarah's eyes brightened. "You will? But you're always so busy with your own projects this time of year."

"Not too busy to help a friend." Margaret glanced around the store, already formulating ideas. "First, let's draw up a floor plan. We can create a one-way traffic flow for the cookie tables —maybe along the perimeter of the store? That way, people won't be bumping into each other."

Sarah's expression brightened. "That could work. And I could designate one corner specifically for the more delicate cookies. Maybe use my nice tablecloth and keep that area a bit more separated."

"Exactly. We can set up a simple check-in table by the door to manage arrivals, or even have timed entry if necessary." Margaret was warming to the challenge. "And you can use it as a marketing opportunity. Offer a special discount that night for holiday book purchases."

"I like how your mind works," Sarah said, her shoulders visibly relaxing. "What about coffee and hot chocolate? Should I offer something special?"

"Maybe add a new flavor to your usual seasonal offerings," Margaret suggested. "Something unique that people can't get anywhere else."

"I could try that gingerbread white hot chocolate recipe I've been saving," Sarah mused. "It would pair well with cookies."

As they continued brainstorming, Sarah's energy seemed to return. They moved from discussing logistics to actually rearranging a few shelves, testing different configurations for the cookie exchange layout.

"This is actually starting to feel manageable," Sarah said as they stepped back to assess their work. "Thank you, Margaret. I appreciate it."

"That's what friends are for," Margaret replied. "Now, how about lunch? You need a proper break."

Sarah checked her watch. "I can't leave the store, but I did bring a huge sandwich. Want half?"

"Sure."

They settled into the comfortable chairs in the reading nook with their impromptu lunch. Margaret took a bite of her sandwich half while Sarah unwrapped hers.

"How's Chris doing these days?" Margaret asked.

A mix of emotions crossed Sarah's face—affection, concern, and something like exasperation. "He's busy with his new venture. The Back Bay Christmas Lights Tour."

"Christmas lights tour?" Margaret repeated. "On his birding boat?"

Sarah nodded. "He's converted the *Blue Heron* for evening tours. He takes people out on the bay to see all the decorated waterfront homes. Some of them go all out with their displays, and they look spectacular from the water."

"That sounds lovely, actually."

"It is," Sarah agreed. "He's added twinkle lights all around the boat railings, plays Christmas music, and even includes a stop at this charming little place on the marina pier for hot chocolate. The whole experience lasts about sixty minutes."

Margaret detected a note of hesitation in Sarah's voice. "But...?"

Sarah sighed. "But it's not quite taking off like he hoped. They've had trouble filling seats most nights. Last Saturday, he only had four passengers on a boat that fits twenty."

"Word of mouth takes time to spread," Margaret offered encouragingly before taking another bite of her sandwich. "The tour could still pick up."

"That's what I keep telling him." Sarah finally took a small bite of her own sandwich, then brushed a crumb from her lap. "The concept is wonderful, but the marketing has been challenging. He made flyers, but they're just sitting in stacks at local businesses. He's not very comfortable with social media, so that's not helping either."

"Is he worried?"

Sarah nodded. "More than he lets on. He invested quite a bit of time decorating the boat and creating marketing materials. He keeps saying it'll pick up closer to Christmas, but I can tell he's concerned."

* * *

"Watch your step here," Nick called over his shoulder as he led Lisa around a pile of lumber stacked near the side of the house. "I picked this up for some indoor shelving projects. It was on sale, so I figured I'd store it here until I'm ready to use it."

Lisa navigated around the wood, taking in the changes to the property. Nick had been working nonstop for the past couple of days while she was tied up with a deadline for her business. In the weeks since he had closed on the bay house, they'd been spending as much time there as possible, slowly transforming the space from a neglected cottage into something that felt like home.

"I can't believe how much you've already done," she said, admiring the progress on the property. Nick had clearly been busy with multiple projects around the cottage.

Nick grinned, giving her a quick kiss. "Wait until you see the deck. I finished the last section yesterday. You haven't seen it since I started sanding it down."

They rounded the corner of the house, and Lisa gasped. The deck, which stretched the entire length of the cottage, had been transformed. Nick had sanded and refinished the worn boards, replaced a few damaged ones, and added solar-powered string lights along the railing. Two Adirondack chairs faced the water, with a small table between them.

"This is gorgeous," Lisa said, running her hand along the smooth railing. "Much better than when we first saw it."

"That's not even the best part," Nick replied, his excitement palpable as he led her down the stairs to the small strip of private beach. "Check this out."

Near the water's edge, Nick had cleared a circular area and ringed it with smooth stones collected from the beach. In the center sat a simple fire pit made of stacked bricks.

"You built the fire pit you talked about," Lisa said softly, remembering their conversation from that night on the beach when Nick was still waiting to hear if his offer had been accepted.

"I promised I would," he replied, his eyes meeting hers for a moment before he looked back at his handiwork. "It's not fancy, but it works. I tested it out last weekend."

"It's perfect," Lisa assured him. "I can already imagine

sitting out here at night with the fire going, listening to the water lapping against the shore."

A smile tugged at the corner of Nick's mouth. "That's exactly what I was thinking." He glanced toward the side of the property. "I've got something else to show you. Come on."

He led her to the detached garage at the side of the property. Nick paused when he noticed the large wooden door was already cracked open a few inches.

"That's strange," he said, pulling it wider. "I'm sure I closed this completely when I left yesterday."

Lisa's eyes widened as the door glided fully along its track. The once-empty garage had been transformed into a surprisingly organized space. Nick had installed a solid workbench along the back wall, with his oyster-farming tools hanging neatly on a pegboard above it. His prized surfboards were mounted on wall brackets, and several fishing rods were displayed in a custom rack he'd built along one side. Boxes labeled with their contents were stacked neatly against another wall, with a few pieces of furniture—a coffee table, two bar stools, and a small bookcase—lined up beside them. In the corner nearest the door, two old beach chairs flanked a small table made from a wooden crate, creating a cozy makeshift sitting area.

"Nick, this is amazing!" she exclaimed, stepping inside. "You've turned it into a real workshop... and a hangout spot."

Nick beamed with pride, then hesitated, scanning the garage. "That's weird."

"What is?" Lisa asked, following his gaze.

"The outdoor cushions for the deck chairs. I bought them last week—blue-and-white-striped ones. I could have sworn I left them right there." He pointed to an empty space next to a stack of boxes.

"Maybe you left them in your truck?" Lisa suggested.

Nick shook his head. "No, I definitely brought them in here. I remember thinking I should keep them protected until I waterproof the deck furniture." He walked around the garage, looking behind boxes and under a tarp covering what appeared to be fishing gear.

"They're not here," he said finally, puzzled. "Could I have taken them back to my other place without remembering?"

Lisa shrugged. "You've been going back and forth so much, it's possible you got mixed up."

"Maybe," Nick conceded, though he didn't sound convinced. "Let's check the house. Maybe I brought them inside instead."

Nick closed the garage door, and they headed into the cottage. The interior was still mostly empty, with just a few essential pieces of furniture—a small dining table with chairs, a comfortable new couch, and a bed in the master bedroom.

"I'll check the closets," Nick said, disappearing down the hallway.

Lisa wandered into the kitchen, which was small but functional with solid wood cabinets and a butcher-block island. She opened a few cupboards, not really expecting to find outdoor cushions there but curious to see what Nick had already moved in. Aside from a few plates, cups, and basic cooking supplies, the cupboards were empty.

"Not in the bedroom or hall closet," Nick called from the other room. "This is bizarre."

He emerged from the hallway, looking perplexed. "I specifically remember putting those cushions in the garage last Tuesday after work. I stopped by my place to check on my parents and pick up a few things, then came here before dark and unloaded everything."

"Maybe they'll turn up," Lisa said, trying to be reassuring. "What else do you want to show me?"

Nick's expression cleared. "Right! I set up a bird feeder on the deck. The previous owners left a shepherd's hook, and I thought it would be nice to—" He broke off as he stepped back onto the deck, his brow furrowing again.

"What now?" Lisa asked, following him outside.

"My gloves," Nick said, pointing to the railing. "I left a pair of winter gloves right here yesterday when I was cleaning the gutters. It got warm, so I took them off and set them on the railing. I meant to grab them before I left, but I forgot."

Lisa looked where he was pointing. The railing was bare. "Maybe the wind blew them off?"

"Maybe," Nick said, walking to the edge of the deck and looking down. "But I don't see them in the yard."

He jogged down the stairs and began scanning the ground around the deck, searching for the missing gloves.

"What color were they?" Lisa called, joining the search.

"Gray with black palms. They're my work gloves, so they're pretty distinctive."

They circled the entire property, checking under bushes and even down on the beach, but the gloves were nowhere to be found.

"This doesn't make sense," Nick said, running a hand through his hair in frustration. "First the cushions, now the gloves."

"Is anything else missing?" Lisa asked.

Nick looked around thoughtfully. "I don't know. Let me check a few things."

He walked to the corner of the yard. "I put three solar landscape lights here two days ago," he said, pointing to an empty patch of soil with small holes where something had been removed. "They're gone too."

Lisa crossed her arms. "That's definitely suspicious. Anything else?"

Nick ran a hand through his hair. "That's all I've noticed so far, but who knows what else might be missing? I haven't been keeping careful track of everything I've brought over."

"Okay, this is officially creepy," Lisa said, wrapping her arms around herself despite the mild temperature. "Do you think someone's stealing from you?"

Nick's face grew serious. "It's starting to look that way. But who? There are only two other houses within a quarter-mile, and both owners are snowbirds who won't be back until spring."

"Could be neighborhood kids," Lisa suggested. "Maybe they're using this place as a hangout when you're not here and taking things as souvenirs."

"Possibly," Nick agreed. "Though how would they know when I'm not here? I've been coming at different times, sometimes early morning, sometimes after work."

They went back inside, and Nick slumped onto the couch, his earlier excitement replaced by concern. "I've been bringing things over gradually to make the move easier, but now I'm worried anything I leave might disappear."

Lisa sat beside him, thinking. "What about setting up a camera? One of those trail cams that activate when there's movement. You could attach it to a tree facing the house."

Nick perked up at the suggestion. "That's not a bad idea."

"It would at least tell you if it's people or something else entirely," Lisa pointed out.

"What other explanation could there be? The wind couldn't have taken those garden lights—they were pushed into the soil. And the cushions were inside the garage."

Lisa shrugged. "I don't know. It's definitely strange. Maybe there's something we're not thinking of."

Nick stood up and began pacing. "Should I report this to the police? It's theft, technically."

"I'm not sure they'd do much about some missing cushions and garden lights," Lisa said. "Might be better to gather evidence first with the camera. Then if it continues or something more valuable goes missing, you'll have something to show them."

Nick nodded reluctantly. "You're right. I'll pick up a camera tomorrow morning."

Nick stopped pacing and looked at her, a new worry

crossing his face. "What if this keeps happening after I move in? What if things start disappearing from inside the house?"

Lisa stood and placed a reassuring hand on his arm. "Let's not get ahead of ourselves. First, we need to find out what's happening. One step at a time."

Nick took a deep breath and nodded. "You're right. Thanks for talking me down."

"That's what I'm here for," Lisa said with a small smile. "So when are we setting up our stakeout?"

"Stakeout?" Nick repeated, confused.

"Well, we need to catch this mysterious thief, don't we? I volunteer to help with surveillance duty."

A grin slowly spread across Nick's face. "Detective Lisa on the case. I like it."

"We could take shifts," she continued, warming to the idea. "Set up the trail cam, but also do some in-person surveillance. Bring thermoses of coffee, binoculars, the whole works."

Nick laughed, his earlier frustration fading. "You've clearly thought this through."

"I've watched a lot of cop shows," Lisa admitted with a grin. "Though usually their stakeouts involve donuts. We should definitely include donuts."

"Donuts, coffee, and a mystery to solve," Nick mused. "Not exactly how I imagined spending my first few weeks at the new place, but I suppose it could be worse."

Lisa raised an eyebrow. "How so?"

"Well," Nick said, "at least we're dealing with a petty thief and not major renovation problems. No leaky roof, no faulty wiring, no octopus shower tiles."

Lisa burst out laughing at the memory of the strange bathroom from the second house they had viewed. "Small blessings," she agreed. "Though I have to say, that octopus shower had a certain... charm."

"Is that what we're calling it?" Nick retorted with a smirk.

They spent the next hour making plans for their

surveillance operation. Nick would get the trail camera and set it up facing the deck and garage area. They decided to do some surveillance together, turning the stakeout into something fun rather than a chore. On a piece of paper, they drew up a crude map of the property, marking the locations where items had disappeared.

As the afternoon light began to fade, they sat on the deck, looking out at the bay. Despite the mystery of the missing items, Nick couldn't help but feel content. The house was coming together, slowly but surely. And having Lisa here, helping him, making him laugh even when he was frustrated... it felt right. Still, as he gazed out over the water, his mind kept circling back to the strange disappearances. Who was taking his things, and why?

CHAPTER FIVE

The familiar path through the woods behind their property felt different in the early evening, shadows lengthening between the bare branches as Margaret and Dave made their way toward the Wilson Christmas tree farm. Margaret pulled her scarf tighter against the chilly air, noting how the temperature had dropped considerably since the sun disappeared behind the tree line.

"I still can't get over how close this place is," she said as they emerged from the dense woods into the towering evergreens that marked the edge of Tom's property. "We've lived here for years, and we never knew it was here."

Dave chuckled, adjusting his flashlight beam to illuminate the path ahead. "You can see how we missed it all this time. From a distance, these evergreens just blend right in with all the tall oaks and maples on our side of the property line."

As they walked deeper into the farm, the glow of vehicle headlights and the warm yellow circles cast by a few scattered work lamps came into view through the trees. Margaret could make out the silhouettes of families moving between the rows of evergreens, their flashlight beams dancing like fireflies in the gathering dusk.

"Look at all these people," Margaret said, watching as a father helped his young daughter drag a handsaw through the base of a Fraser fir while his wife held a flashlight steady. "I had no idea the farm was this busy."

They could see cars parked in a rough semicircle near Tom's cabin: a weathered pickup truck, a minivan, and a sedan. Their headlights added to the patchwork of illumination that lit the immediate area. As they stepped from the wooded path onto the farm property, the evening air carried the sounds of families at work. Children's laughter mixed with the steady rhythm of handsaws cutting through wood, and the occasional call of "This one's perfect!" echoed from somewhere among the trees.

Unlike the brightly lit tree lots in town with their neat rows of pre-cut trees and string lights, this place had a timeless quality. Customers wandered the rows with flashlights, examining trees by narrow beams of light, debating the merits of various specimens before making their selections and cutting them down with handsaws Tom provided.

Margaret spotted Tom near the cabin, his silver hair catching the light from a nearby work lamp as he helped an elderly couple navigate their freshly cut tree toward their sedan.

"Mr. Wilson!" Dave called as they approached.

Tom looked up from securing the tree to the sedan's roof and broke into a broad smile. "Dave! Margaret! Wonderful to see you both. As you can see, we're having quite the evening."

Two young men emerged from between the rows of trees, each carrying one end of a particularly large blue spruce. Even in the dim light, Margaret could see the family resemblance—both had Tom's build and his bright-blue eyes, though their hair was brown.

"These are my grandsons," Tom said with obvious pride as the young men approached. "Jake and Tyler. Boys, these are my new neighbors I was telling you about—Dave and Margaret."

The older of the two, who appeared to be in his early twenties, extended his hand. "Jake Wilson. Pleasure to meet you." His grip was firm, his hands rough from outdoor work despite his obvious youth.

"And I'm Tyler," the younger one added with a grin that was pure Tom Wilson. "Grandpa mentioned you're the neighbors who discovered the farm."

A family with three young children approached, the parents looking slightly overwhelmed as they tried to manage flashlights, a handsaw, and their excited offspring all at once. Tom immediately moved to help them, but Margaret could see the busy evening was taking its toll.

"Tom," Margaret said, "would you mind if Dave and I helped out tonight? It looks like you could use some extra hands."

Tom paused, clearly surprised by the offer. "Oh, that's very kind, but I couldn't ask you to—"

"You're not asking," Dave interrupted with a smile. "We're offering. We'd love to help."

Jake and Tyler exchanged a glance before Jake spoke up. "Actually, Grandpa, that would be great. We could definitely use the extra hands tonight."

Tom looked around at the scattered groups of customers still moving between the trees, clearly weighing his pride against practical necessity. Finally, he nodded. "Well, if you're sure you don't mind..."

"We're sure," Margaret said firmly. "Just tell us what to do."

For the next two hours, Margaret and Dave threw themselves into the rhythm of the Christmas tree farm. Dave quickly proved himself adept at helping customers maneuver their chosen trees out of the tight rows and assisting with the cutting when someone's enthusiasm exceeded their physical capabilities. Margaret found herself drawn to the more social aspects of the operation, helping families wrap their trees in netting and managing the wonderfully informal payment system that consisted of a metal cashbox and a notebook where Tom recorded each sale in his careful handwriting.

"Twelve-foot Fraser fir," she wrote in the notebook as a young couple counted out bills for their towering tree. "That's going to be absolutely gorgeous."

The woman beamed. "It's our first Christmas in our new house. We wanted something really special."

"You chose well," Margaret assured her, watching as Dave and Jake worked together to secure the massive tree to the couple's SUV. "Mr. Wilson grows the most beautiful trees I've ever seen."

As the evening progressed, Margaret began to understand the unique appeal of the Wilson farm. There was something almost ceremonial about the process of walking among the trees with only a flashlight, taking time to examine each specimen carefully before making a selection. Unlike the festive farms with their hayrides, hot chocolate stands, and gift shops —which had their own charm—this place offered something different entirely. Here, the focus was purely on the trees themselves and the quiet ritual of choosing one. The darkness beyond each glowing circle made the farm feel like a true forest, where visitors could lose themselves in the simple act of finding the perfect tree without distraction. The rich scent of pine and earth filled the air, and the soft crunch of fallen needles underfoot added to the authentic woodland experience. The families she helped seemed to relish the adventure of it all—children racing between rows with dancing beams of light, parents debating the relative merits of different varieties, everyone working together to cut down their chosen tree as if they were true woodsmen claiming their prize from the wild.

"No credit cards?" asked a father as he pulled cash from his wallet for a beautiful white pine.

"Never needed 'em," Tom replied with a chuckle. "Cash works just fine for us. Always has."

Margaret watched the man count out the bills without complaint, struck by how readily people adapted to the farm's traditional approach. There was something refreshing about the simplicity—just Tom's careful notations in his handwritten ledger and the honor system that worked perfectly for his loyal customer base.

As the last of the evening's customers secured their trees and drove away, their taillights disappearing down the dark dirt road, Jake and Tyler went to close the gate at the road entrance.

A voice called from the direction of the cabin. "Thomas Wilson, you'd better not be working those nice neighbors of ours too hard!"

Margaret turned to see a petite woman emerging from the cabin, her silver hair caught up in a loose bun and her arms laden with a large thermos and a basket. Even in the dim light from the work lamps, her resemblance to Nanette from the porch photograph was unmistakable.

"That would be my wife," Tom said with obvious affection as the woman approached. "Nanette, come meet Dave and Margaret."

Nanette Wilson made her way over to them, set down her burdens, and immediately enveloped Margaret in a warm hug, as if they were old friends rather than strangers meeting for the first time. "I'm so sorry I missed you when you stopped by last week," she said, her voice friendly and welcoming. "I was in town dealing with a dental appointment. You know how these things go."

"It's wonderful to meet you," Margaret replied, genuinely charmed by the woman's immediate warmth.

Nanette turned to Dave, subjecting him to the same enthusiastic greeting. "And you must be Dave. I saw you helping families with their trees from the kitchen window. What a wonderful thing to do."

"We've enjoyed every minute of it," Dave assured her. "It's a beautiful place you have here."

"Forty years I've been telling him he needs better lighting out here," Nanette said with a fond glance at her husband, "and forty years he's been telling me that flashlights and headlights work just fine."

Tom chuckled. "If it's not broken, why fix it?"

"Because your customers shouldn't need to navigate your farm like they're on a wilderness expedition," Nanette replied, but her tone was affectionate rather than critical. "Though I'll admit, the children do seem to love the adventure of it all."

She gestured toward the thermos and basket she had brought. "I made hot cider—thought everyone could use something warm after working in this cold." She looked directly at Margaret and Dave. "And I won't hear any arguments about you two heading home without joining us for dinner. I've got pot roast in the oven, and there's more than enough for everyone."

Margaret glanced at Dave, who nodded almost imperceptibly. Harper and Abby were with their father for his overnight, so they had the evening free. "That's incredibly kind of you," she said. "Are you sure we wouldn't be imposing?"

"Imposing?" Nanette laughed, a sound like silver bells in the crisp air. "Honey, you just spent your evening helping my stubborn husband instead of relaxing at home after your own long day. The least I can do is feed you properly."

Jake and Tyler had finished shutting down the work lamps and securing the handsaws for the night. As they gathered around Nanette's thermos of cider, passing around steaming cups, Margaret found herself thinking about how different this was from any other business operation she had ever encountered. The farm felt less like a commercial enterprise and more like an extended family gathering, with customers treated as welcomed guests rather than transactions to be processed.

"Grandma makes the best pot roast in Cape May County," Tyler announced, wrapping his cold hands around his cup of cider.

"Don't oversell it," Nanette chided, but she looked pleased. "Though I will say, after forty years of practice, I've gotten fairly good at it."

As they made their way toward the cabin, Margaret caught Dave's eye in the golden light spilling from the windows. She could see her own thoughts reflected in his expression—this place, these people, represented something increasingly rare in their modern world. The Wilson farm operated on principles of trust, tradition, and genuine human connection that seemed almost miraculous in their simplicity.

The cabin's interior was as cozy and welcoming as Margaret had imagined. The main room combined kitchen, dining, and living areas in an open layout that felt spacious despite the modest square footage. A stone fireplace dominated one wall, its hearth crackling with split oak, while the kitchen area featured vintage appliances and worn wooden countertops that spoke of decades of good use. The dining table, clearly handmade from pine, was already set for six.

"Sit, sit," Nanette insisted, guiding them toward chairs while she bustled around the kitchen. "Tom, help me get this food on the table before everything gets cold."

The meal that followed was the kind of comfort food Margaret associated with her own grandmother's kitchen—tender pot roast with carrots and onions, mashed potatoes with real butter, fresh dinner rolls that were still warm from the oven, and green beans that Nanette had prepared with care.

"This is incredible," Dave said after his first bite. "I haven't had pot roast this good in a long time."

Nanette beamed with pleasure. "There's nothing fancy

about it—just good ingredients and taking the time to do it right."

As they ate, the conversation flowed naturally from topic to topic. Jake and Tyler shared stories of growing up on the farm, spending their Christmas breaks from school helping with the busy season and learning the business from their grandfather.

"I remember when I was about eight," Jake said, cutting into his pot roast, "Grandpa let me help a family choose their tree for the first time. I was so nervous I could barely hold the flashlight steady."

"He was terrified he'd recommend a tree with a bald spot," Tyler added with a grin. "Spent twenty minutes examining every branch."

"Better safe than sorry," Tom said with obvious pride. "Jake's got a good eye for trees now. Both boys do."

"What are you studying in school?" Margaret asked, genuinely curious about these young men who seemed so comfortable with both hard physical work and the social aspects of running a family business.

"I'm finishing up my finance degree at Rutgers," Jake replied. "Senior year. Been interning with an investment firm in Philadelphia."

"And I'm studying engineering at Penn State," Tyler added. "Freshman year. Focusing on environmental systems design. We're home for winter break, so we always help Grandpa with the Christmas rush."

Dave nodded approvingly. "Those are both excellent fields. Do you see yourselves eventually taking over the farm alongside your careers?"

An awkward silence fell over the table. Jake and Tyler exchanged a glance, and Margaret noticed Tom's expression grow more serious.

"That's... well, that's part of the challenge we're facing," Tom said carefully. "The boys have worked hard to build their own futures. Jake's got a job offer in Philadelphia after graduation, and Tyler's got his sights set on graduate school and then work with an environmental consulting firm."

"It's not that we don't love this place," Jake said quickly, as if he was worried they might have given offense. "Growing up here was incredible. Some of my best memories are of Christmas seasons on the farm."

"But it's hard to see how we could make a living from it," Tyler added. "Grandpa and Grandma have done an amazing job building something special here, but it's not... well, it's not really scalable. And frankly, neither of us has the passion for it that they do."

Tom nodded slowly. "My kids aren't interested either. Sarah's got her real estate business, and Tommy Jr.—that's Jake and Tyler's dad—he's been with the county planning department for twenty years. They help out when they can, but they've got their own lives and careers."

Margaret felt a pang of sadness at the honesty in Tom's voice. She could see how much the farm meant to Tom and Nanette, and the weight of knowing their life's work wouldn't continue in the family must be difficult to bear.

"That's completely understandable," Dave said diplomatically. "You have to follow your own paths."

Nanette reached over and squeezed Jake's hand. "We're proud of both of you boys, no matter what you choose to do. This farm has been a wonderful life for us, but that doesn't mean it's the right choice for everyone."

"Still," Tom said quietly, "it does make the decision about what to do with the place more pressing. At my age, these old knees aren't getting any better."

"That developer still calling?" Jake asked.

Tom nodded grimly. "Twice a week, like clockwork. They're persistent, I'll give them that."

"Forty-two houses, they're saying," Nanette added with barely concealed distaste. "They'd clear-cut everything except maybe a few of the biggest trees for 'aesthetic purposes.'" She made air quotes around the phrase.

"The money would be good," Tom admitted. "Better than good, actually. Would set us up nicely for retirement and leave something substantial for the boys and their parents."

"But?" Dave prompted, sensing there was more to the story.

Tom sighed, looking out the window toward the darkened tree farm. "But I've spent fifty years of my life growing those trees. Every one of them planted by either my father or myself. The thought of watching them all get bulldozed..." He shook his head. "I know it's sentimental, but this place is more than just a business to me. It's a piece of Cape May history."

"People have been coming here for their Christmas trees for generations," Nanette added. "Some of our customers are grandparents now who came here as children with their own parents. It feels like we'd be breaking a trust."

Margaret found herself leaning forward, drawn into the family's dilemma. "Have you considered other options? Besides the developer, I mean?"

"We've thought about it," Tom replied. "Some of our regular customers have asked if we'd consider selling to someone who would keep it operating as is, but honestly, we haven't had any serious inquiries along those lines."

The conversation was interrupted by the ringing of a phone mounted on the kitchen wall. Tom rose stiffly from his chair to answer it.

"Wilson Christmas Trees," he said, his voice taking on the friendly, professional tone Margaret had come to associate with his customer interactions. "Oh, hello, Mrs. Doyle. Yes, we're still open for the season... This Saturday would be perfect. Same time as usual? Wonderful. We'll see you then."

He hung up and returned to the table with a smile. "Mrs. Doyle and her family. They've been coming here for fifteen years, always the Saturday before Christmas. Her grandson just got engaged, so this year they're picking out their first tree as a couple."

"See what I mean?" Nanette said to Margaret and Dave. "These aren't just customers—they're part of our extended family. How do you put a price on that?"

As the evening wound down and they prepared to head home, Margaret found herself thinking about the Wilson family's dilemma. The farm represented something increasingly rare—a business built on personal relationships and traditional values rather than efficiency and profit margins. The thought of it being replaced by yet another cookie-cutter subdivision filled her with an unexpected sense of loss.

"Thank you for dinner," she said as Nanette walked them to the door. "And for sharing your evening with us. We really enjoyed meeting you."

"The pleasure was all ours," Nanette replied with a smile. "It's wonderful to have neighbors who appreciate what this place is all about."

As they walked home along the dark dirt road, Margaret looked back at the shadowy forms of the evergreens they were leaving behind. Somewhere in those rows of trees was the solution to the Wilson family's problem—she was sure of it. The challenge would be figuring out what that solution looked like.

* * *

As their laughter finally subsided, Liz and Greg found themselves sitting cross-legged on the floor among the scattered preschool furniture, looking completely out of place in the miniature world surrounding them. Greg picked up one of the tiny yellow chairs, turning it over in his hands with a rueful smile.

"You know what?" he said, setting the chair down carefully. "Maybe this is the universe telling us something."

Liz raised an eyebrow, reaching for a hot-pink feather boa

that had somehow wound up draped across a miniature table. "That we should open a daycare instead of a café?"

"That we've been pushing ourselves too hard," Greg replied, his voice growing more serious. "Look at us, Liz. When's the last time we had a full night's sleep? Or ate dinner together without discussing contractors and permits?"

Liz considered this, absently twirling the feather boa around her finger. The exhaustion she'd been fighting for weeks seemed to settle more heavily on her shoulders as she acknowledged it. "You're right. I've been so focused on our spring opening that I forgot we don't actually need to have everything perfect by Christmas."

Greg nodded, glancing around at the chaos surrounding them. "What if we just... stopped? For the holidays, I mean. Put everything on hold until January."

The suggestion hung in the air between them, and Liz felt something inside her chest loosen—a tension she hadn't even realized she'd been carrying. "We could do that," she said slowly. "There's really no rush."

Greg stood up, brushing dust off his jeans, and walked over to the large chalkboard they'd mounted on the wall for planning purposes. He picked up a piece of chalk and began writing in his neat handwriting.

"January 3rd," he said aloud as he wrote. "Resolve delivery issues."

"January 10th," Liz added, watching him write. "Furniture delivery and setup."

"January 15th," Greg continued. "Menu planning and pricing."

They continued adding items to the timeline, each task finding its proper place in the coming months.

Liz joined him at the chalkboard, taking the chalk to add her own notes. "February 1st—staff hiring. February 15th—finalize décor and fixtures."

"February 20th—marketing launch," Greg added. "March

1st—staff training and menu testing. March 30th—grand opening."

They stepped back to survey their new timeline, and Greg shook his head with amazement. "Look at that. We actually have time."

"Plenty of time," Liz agreed. The relief was palpable, like taking off shoes that had been too tight all day. "I can't believe we were trying to cram all of this into December."

Greg pulled out his phone and dialed a familiar number. "Hey, Steven," he said when one of their sons answered. "Change of plans. Mom and I will be home for dinner after all... Yes, tonight... No, everything's fine. We just decided to take a break from the store prep... We'll pick up some Chinese food on our way home. See you in an hour."

As Greg ended the call, Liz was already gathering up the more inappropriate bachelorette party items and placing them back in their boxes. "I suppose we should secure all this until we can return it," she said, holding up a particularly scandalous drinking straw. "Though I have to admit, some of these are pretty creative."

They spent the next twenty minutes boxing up the party supplies and stacking them in a corner, then covering the pallets of children's furniture with the plastic tarps they'd been using to protect their work surfaces. The space still looked completely ridiculous, but at least the most out-of-place items were hidden from view.

"Ready?" Greg asked, keys in hand as they stood by the front door.

Liz took one last look around Furnish & Feast, taking it all in, and the progress they'd made despite the day's setbacks. "You know what? I think this might be exactly what we needed."

"The wrong deliveries?"

"The reminder that we don't have to do everything at

once," she clarified. "That it's okay to slow down and enjoy the season."

Greg flipped off the lights and held the door open for her. "Christmas movies tonight?"

"Definitely. The cheesier the better." Liz stepped out onto the sidewalk, breathing in the winter air. "It'll be nice to just relax for once."

"I can't remember the last time we had a whole evening free," Greg agreed.

As they walked to their car, Greg slipped his arm around Liz's shoulders. "Well, this has been an adventure."

Thirty minutes later, they were settled on their living room couch with Steven and Michael, a collection of Chinese takeout containers spread across the coffee table. The gas fireplace radiated comforting heat across the room, and the first Christmas movie of the evening was already queued up on the television.

"So let me get this straight," Steven said, reaching for another egg roll. "You got furniture for toddlers and party supplies for brides?"

"That's the simplified version," Greg replied, passing the lo mein to Michael.

"And you're just going to leave it there until January?" Michael asked, clearly delighted by the absurdity of the situation.

"What else can we do?" Liz shrugged. "Sometimes you just have to roll with it."

As the opening credits of their chosen movie began to play, Liz settled back against the couch cushions, feeling more relaxed than she had in weeks. The stress of delivery schedules and timeline pressures suddenly seemed manageable, pushed safely into the future where it belonged.

Greg caught her eye and smiled, the same relieved expression she knew was on her own face. Sometimes the best-laid plans needed to be derailed, if only to remind you what really mattered. And right now, surrounded by her family, with hot chocolate warming her hands and Christmas lights twinkling outside the window, Liz couldn't think of anywhere else she'd rather be. Still, part of her was excited about what lay ahead—Furnish & Feast would be everything they'd dreamed of, when the time was right.

CHAPTER SIX

Dale stood at the restaurant window, arms folded across his chest, watching the Christmas carnival in full swing. The flashing lights from the Ferris wheel cast colorful shadows across his face as he surveyed what had become of their normally quiet street. Where there had once been a peaceful view of the Cape May evening, there was now a chaotic spectacle of crowds, blinking lights, and constant motion.

"Unbelievable," he muttered, squinting as the Ferris wheel completed another rotation.

What bothered him most wasn't just the visual intrusion but the practical problems the carnival had created. The street parking, already at a premium in this part of town, was completely overtaken by carnival-goers. The few spots directly in front of Donna's Restaurant, which they had always counted on for their older clientele who couldn't walk far, were now filled with cars whose occupants had no intention of dining with them.

Dale watched as the Hendersons pulled up in their familiar blue sedan—the older couple who came in weekly for their standing date night. He saw Mrs. Henderson point toward their usual parking spot in front of the restaurant, now occupied by a minivan. Mr. Henderson circled the block twice, Mrs. Henderson turning this way and that as they searched for somewhere to park. Finally, Dale watched helplessly as they drove away, Mrs. Henderson's disappointed face visible through the passenger window.

His stomach tightened. The Hendersons had been coming to Donna's Restaurant weekly for the past year. They always ordered the same thing—chicken marsala for her, salmon for him, and they always split a piece of tiramisu. Mrs. Henderson had mobility issues and couldn't walk more than a few yards, which was why they always counted on that front parking spot. That was the third potential table he'd seen leave in the past hour alone, but losing the Hendersons felt personal.

The front door opened, letting in a blast of Christmas music so loud that several diners looked up from their meals with visible annoyance. A teenage boy in a puffy winter coat stepped halfway inside.

"Bathroom?" he asked, not bothering with pleasantries.

Dale uncrossed his arms and stepped toward him. "I'm sorry, but our restrooms are for customers only."

The boy rolled his eyes. "Come on, man. The port-a-potties at the carnival have lines like twenty people deep."

"I understand, but—"

"Whatever," the boy said, already backing out the door. "The place across the street let me use theirs."

As the door closed, Dale made a mental note to call Giorgio's and warn them about becoming the neighborhood bathroom. This was the eighth non-customer who'd come in asking to use their facilities in the past two hours alone.

He returned to his position by the window, watching as a gust of wind caught several napkins and an empty popcorn container from the carnival and blew them directly onto their outdoor seating area. The patio was closed for the season, but it still reflected on their establishment. He would need to send someone out to clean up again before the night was over.

The Christmas music from the carnival speakers swelled suddenly. "Jingle Bell Rock" for what had to be the fifth time that evening. Dale saw an older couple at table seven exchange glances before the husband beckoned him over.

"I'm sorry," the man said when Dale approached, "but we can barely hear each other across the table. Is there anything you can do about that music?"

Dale forced a smile. "I apologize for the inconvenience. I've spoken with the carnival organizers about the volume, but unfortunately, they haven't been willing to turn it down."

The wife sighed. "We can't even have a conversation."

"I understand. Let me speak with the kitchen about expediting your entrées." Dale walked away, his smile fading the moment his back was turned. This was exactly what he'd feared. He'd already watched several potential customers drive away earlier in the evening due to the parking situation. Now the noise was threatening to drive away the customers who had actually made it inside.

In the kitchen, Dale checked on the orders, then leaned against the wall, closing his eyes briefly. The dinner service was limping along at half capacity. At this rate, they might as well close early and cut their losses until the carnival packed up and left town. More days of this stretched ahead. The thought made his head pound worse than the Christmas music.

"Another bathroom seeker?" Donna asked, appearing beside him with a tray of appetizers.

"Number eight," Dale confirmed. "And the couple at table seven are about to walk out because they can't hear each other over 'Jingle Bell Rock.'"

Donna set down her plate and studied him. "You're in full storm-cloud mode."

"Can you blame me? This carnival is killing us."

"It's only been open for a couple days."

"And it's already a disaster," Dale insisted. "We should just close early and—"

Donna took his arm and pulled him into the small office at the back of the kitchen, closing the door behind them. The music from outside was slightly muffled in here, though still audible.

"Listen to me," she said, placing her hands on his shoulders. "We're not closing early, and we're not going to spend the rest of the week sulking while we lose business."

Dale started to protest, but she held up a hand to stop him.

"If we can't beat them, we need to join them."

"What are you talking about?"

A slow smile spread across Donna's face. "I've been thinking about this all day. The carnival is bringing hundreds of people right to our doorstep. Instead of seeing them as the enemy, what if we found a way to turn them into customers?"

Dale considered this. "They're not exactly our target demographic. They're here for cotton candy and carnival games, not fine dining."

"So we adjust," Donna said simply. "Just temporarily. What if we created some carnival-inspired specials? High-end versions of carnival food that might entice them to step inside?"

"Like what?"

Donna's eyes lit up with enthusiasm. "Gourmet fried Oreos with Madagascar vanilla bean ice cream. Upscale corn dogs made with our housemade sausage and a honey mustard aioli. Maybe a fancy hot chocolate bar with handcrafted marshmallows and flavored whipped creams."

Dale crossed his arms again, but his expression had softened slightly. "That's a major departure from our usual menu."

"It's just for the week," Donna insisted. "We could call it our special 'Carnival Week' menu. Keep our regular items too, of course, but add these special offerings to draw in the carnival crowd."

Dale considered this. The idea wasn't completely without merit. They had the skills and equipment to execute those dishes well, and it might actually appeal to families who wanted something better than carnival food but less formal than their usual fare.

"We could also extend our hours," Donna continued, clearly warming to her idea. "Stay open a bit later to catch the post-ride hungry customers. The carnival closes at eleven, right? What if we offered a special late-night menu from nine to midnight?"

"That would mean restructuring our staffing," Dale pointed out, though he was starting to see the potential in her plan.

"Worth it if it fills tables," Donna countered. "Oh, and my old funnel cake cart is still in our garage. What if we asked the city if we could park it out front for the week? Sell some upscale funnel cakes right at the carnival entrance?"

Dale raised an eyebrow. "You think that old cart still works?"

"Should be fine with a little cleanup," Donna said, squeezing his arm. "Think about it. We could draw people in with the funnel cakes then hand them a menu for the restaurant while they're waiting."

The idea was starting to take shape in Dale's mind, despite his initial resistance. It was a complete pivot from their usual approach, but maybe that was exactly what the situation called for.

"The noise is still going to be an issue," he said, not quite ready to fully concede. "And the parking situation isn't going to improve."

"We can't solve everything," Donna admitted. "But we can try to make the best of it."

Dale looked at her, his frustration gradually giving way to reluctant admiration. Where he saw obstacles, she saw opportunities.

"You're serious about this."

"Dead serious," Donna confirmed. "Look, Dale, we can either spend the rest of the week fighting against something we can't change, or we can adapt and maybe even benefit from it."

Dale took a deep breath and gazed past her to the kitchen beyond, where their staff was dutifully preparing meals for the half-empty dining room.

"Fine," he said finally. "Let's try it your way. But we're going to need to move fast if we want to implement all this."

Donna grinned and reached up to kiss his cheek. "Leave the marketing to me. You start thinking about those gourmet carnival recipes."

As they stepped back into the kitchen, another chorus of "Jingle Bell Rock" filtered through from outside. Dale winced but squared his shoulders. If Donna thought they could turn this situation around, he owed it to her to try.

"I can't believe I'm looking forward to this," Bob said with a chuckle as he held the door of Charlotte's Way Inn open for Judy.

Judy adjusted her scarf and smiled. "You're the one who suggested we come back for karaoke night."

"For the entertainment," Bob clarified, following her into the warmth of the restaurant. "I'm still not volunteering to sing."

The hostess greeted them with a bright smile. "Table for two?"

"Yes, please," Judy replied. "And if possible, we'd like a spot with a good view of where the karaoke happens."

The hostess's eyebrows rose slightly in pleased surprise. "Absolutely! Are you planning to sing tonight?"

"Oh, no," Bob said quickly. "We just enjoy watching."

"Well, you never know. Sometimes the holiday spirit takes over," the hostess said with a wink, collecting two menus. "Follow me."

She led them to a table that was notably better positioned than their previous one—a small two-top with an unobstructed view of the area where the karaoke machine was already set up. The restaurant was busier tonight, with a pleasant buzz of conversation filling the space.

"Perfect," Judy said as they settled in. "We can see everything from here."

Bob studied the menu, looking for something different to try. "I wonder if our singing friend will be back tonight."

"I hope so," Judy replied, scanning the restaurant. "I don't see him yet."

They ordered drinks and their meals—the seafood risotto for Judy, chicken piccata for Bob—and settled in for the evening's entertainment. The karaoke was scheduled to begin earlier tonight, and they'd timed their arrival accordingly.

As they waited for their drinks, the hostess stepped up to the microphone. "Good evening, everyone! Welcome to our Christmas Karaoke Night at Charlotte's Way Inn! Who's ready to spread some holiday cheer with a song?"

The first volunteer was a young man in a business suit who looked like he'd come directly from an office party. His rendition of "Rockin' Around the Christmas Tree" was energetic but painfully off-key. Judy noticed several diners exchanging glances, some visibly wincing at the high notes.

"Ten points for enthusiasm," Bob whispered when their drinks were served, "minus several million for execution."

Next came a middle-aged woman whose "Silent Night" was pleasant but forgettable, followed by a teenage girl who surprised everyone with an impressive version of "Santa Baby" that earned genuine applause.

Throughout the performances, Judy found herself watching the audience as much as the singers. At a table near the bar, a group of friends barely concealed their laughter during a particularly rough performance. An older couple near the window kept exchanging dramatic eye rolls. At another table, a woman leaned toward her companion and whispered something that made them both snicker behind their menus.

"People can be so unkind," Judy murmured to Bob as their meals arrived. "It takes courage to get up there."

"Which is precisely why I'm staying right here in my seat," Bob replied, cutting into his chicken.

Their entrees were delicious, and they ate at a leisurely pace, commenting on each performer between bites. As their plates were being cleared, Judy noticed a familiar figure entering the restaurant.

"Bob," she said softly, nodding toward the door. "He's here."

The older gentleman from their previous visit was being greeted by the hostess, who seemed delighted to see him. He wore a different blazer tonight—a deep burgundy that complemented the season—with the same dignified presence despite his slight stoop. The hostess led him to a small table near the bar.

"I wonder if he'll sing again," Bob said, accepting the dessert menu from their server.

They decided to share a slice of chocolate cake, prolonging their stay. After several more karaoke performances of varying quality, the hostess scanned the room.

"Any other brave souls tonight?"

The older man rose from his seat and made his way toward the karaoke machine. This time, Judy noticed, several regular patrons seemed to recognize him, nudging their companions and turning their attention toward the performance area.

"Good evening," he said into the microphone, his voice smooth and clear. "I think I'll sing 'The Christmas Song' tonight."

As the familiar opening notes of "Chestnuts Roasting on an Open Fire" filled the restaurant, a hush fell over the room. Unlike their previous visit, conversations paused, and silverware was set down as diners turned to listen.

His voice was as beautiful as they remembered. He sang with his eyes open this time, his gaze sweeping across the room, connecting with his audience. As he moved through the familiar melody, he smiled gently, and Judy felt the sincerity behind the words.

When he finished, the applause was immediate and enthusiastic. Several people even offered appreciative whistles and calls of "Bravo!" The man gave a humble nod, clearly pleased by the reception.

As he turned to leave the performance area, his gaze landed on Judy and Bob. A flicker of recognition crossed his face, and after a moment's hesitation, he made his way toward their table.

"Forgive me," he said, stopping beside them, "but weren't you here a few days ago?"

Bob nodded, extending his hand. "We were. Enjoyed your performance then too, though I think more people were paying attention tonight."

The man smiled, accepting Bob's handshake. "May I?" he asked, gesturing to the empty chair at their table.

"Please," Judy said.

"I'm Henry Dawson," he said as he lowered himself carefully into the chair. "Retired now, but I used to sing professionally."

"I knew it," Bob said, looking pleased with himself. "You have a trained voice. I'm Bob, and this is my wife, Judy."

"Lovely to meet you both," Henry replied. "What brings you back to karaoke night? Are you planning to sing?"

Judy laughed softly. "No, no. We just enjoyed the evening last time and thought we'd come back."

"Wonderful," Henry said. "It's nice to see familiar faces."

"Were you with a band?" Bob asked. "Or opera, perhaps?"

Henry chuckled. "Nothing quite so glamorous. I was a jingle singer."

"A jingle singer?" Judy repeated.

"Commercial jingles," Henry explained. "You know those catchy little tunes that get stuck in your head? Coffee brands, food products, department stores. I sang dozens of them through the sixties, seventies, and eighties."

"That's fascinating," Judy said sincerely. "So your voice has probably been heard by millions of people."

"Tens of millions, I'd wager," Henry said, his eyes twinkling. "Though they never knew it was me. I was part of a group of studio singers who made a good living being anonymously famous."

"Any jingles we might recognize?" Bob asked.

Henry's face lit up. "Well, I was the lead vocalist on the old Carrington's Department Store holiday commercials. 'Christmas time at Carrington's, where the magic never ends.'" He sang the line softly, and Judy immediately recognized the jingle from years ago.

"I remember those!" she exclaimed. "They used to run every December when we were younger."

"That was me," Henry said with evident pride. "And I did the bass part for Jersey Fresh Dairy's 'Milk so good, it moo-ves you.'" He dropped his voice to demonstrate, and Bob laughed in recognition.

"Amazing," Bob said. "You were part of the soundtrack of our lives without us knowing it."

Henry nodded, a wistful expression crossing his face. "It was a wonderful career. My wife, Teresa, used to say she couldn't turn on the radio or television without hearing my voice."

"Is your wife here tonight?" Judy asked.

Henry's smile dimmed slightly. "She passed away last spring. Fifty-two years we had together."

"I'm so sorry," Judy said softly.

"Thank you," Henry replied. "It's been difficult. Our children live out west—one in Seattle, one in Denver. They have their own families, their own lives. They invited me to move closer, but this has been our home for forty years."

"Do you live nearby?" Bob asked.

"Just a few blocks from here," Henry said. "I can walk when the weather's decent. That's partly why I started coming to these karaoke nights. Gets me out of the house, gives me something to look forward to."

"Well, your performances certainly give us something to look forward to as well," Judy said.

Henry smiled at her. "The holidays can be especially lonely. Teresa loved Christmas—the music, the decorations, all of it. Singing these songs helps me feel connected to her, somehow."

There was a moment of comfortable silence before Henry leaned forward slightly.

"You know," he said, "you should give it a try yourselves."

Bob shook his head immediately. "Oh, no. I couldn't possibly."

"Everyone can sing," Henry insisted gently. "Some better than others, certainly, but everyone has a voice."

"Mine is best kept in the shower," Bob replied with a chuckle.

"What about you, Judy?" Henry asked. "Would you consider it?"

Judy felt a flutter of anxiety at the thought. "I don't think so. I haven't sung in public since the church choir, decades ago."

"I could sing with you," Henry offered. "A duet is much less intimidating. 'Baby, It's Cold Outside,' perhaps, or 'Winter Wonderland'?"

Judy smiled at his enthusiasm but shook her head. "It's very kind of you to offer, but I think I prefer being in the audience."

"Well, the offer stands," Henry said, not pushing further. "For both of you."

As the hostess announced the final call for karaoke

performers, Henry rose from the table. "I should be going. It was a pleasure meeting you both."

"The pleasure was ours," Bob replied. "Will you be here again soon?"

"I try to come whenever they have karaoke," Henry confirmed. "It's become my little tradition."

He reached into his pocket and pulled out a small notepad and pen. After writing something down, he tore off the page and placed it on their table.

"My telephone number," he explained. "In case you change your mind about singing." His eyes twinkled as he added, "Or if you'd just like company for coffee sometime. At my age, new friends are a precious gift."

Judy felt touched by the gesture. "Thank you, Henry. We might take you up on that."

Henry nodded, then added with a slight smile, "Call me if you change your mind about singing. Everyone should sing at Christmas, even if just once."

With a small wave, he made his way toward the exit, stopping briefly to thank the hostess before disappearing into the December night.

Bob picked up the piece of paper, looking at the neat, slightly shaky handwriting. "What do you think?"

Judy watched the door where Henry had exited, thinking about his fifty-two years of marriage, his distant children, and the loneliness he'd acknowledged but seemed determined to combat with music and connection.

"I think," she said slowly, "that we might need to practice a Christmas carol or two."

Bob raised an eyebrow. "Really?"

Judy shrugged, a small smile playing at her lips. "As Henry said, everyone should sing at Christmas."

Bob tucked the piece of paper carefully into his wallet. "We'll see."

CHAPTER SEVEN

Sarah stood back, hands on her hips, surveying what had once been her bookstore. The Book Nook had undergone a remarkable transformation since she'd closed early at four o'clock. Gone was the usual arrangement of browsing tables and featured displays. Instead, the central space now hosted a series of rectangular tables draped in red and green cloths, forming a continuous path around the perimeter of the store.

Around her, participants bustled about making final preparations. Two women stretched tablecloths and smoothed wrinkles, while a man helped arrange the cookie serving areas. Someone's teenage daughter carefully positioned small Christmas trees as centerpieces, and the sound of cheerful chatter filled the air as everyone worked together.

"I think we've actually pulled this off," Sarah said, adjusting a small wreath hanging from one of the shelves. The cookie tables had been arranged throughout the available floor space, forming a path around the perimeter of the store and organized by type—chocolate varieties including buckeyes and chocolate chip on one table, traditional holiday favorites like snickerdoodles and sugar cookies on another, international specialties on a third, and so on.

Margaret looked up from the check-in table near the entrance, where she was setting out name cards. "It looks fantastic. No one would guess this was a last-minute venue change."

The space felt intimate yet festive. White Christmas lights twinkled along the ceiling, and sprigs of holly and pine adorned strategic spots throughout the store. The coffee counter had been transformed into a beverage station, complete with Sarah's special gingerbread white hot chocolate, regular hot chocolate, and coffee. The scent of cinnamon and vanilla filled the air.

"Those vintage Christmas books were the perfect touch," Margaret noted, pointing to where Sarah had displayed several beautifully illustrated holiday classics on elevated stands interspersed among the cookie tables. The collection from an estate sale she'd attended last week—editions from the 1930s through the 1950s with their charming illustrated covers—added an authentic nostalgic element to the decor.

"I just hope no one gets cookie crumbs on them," Sarah fretted, straightening a first-edition "Night Before Christmas" with hand-colored illustrations.

"That's why we put them up high," Margaret reassured her.

The doorbell jingled, and both women turned.

"Am I too early?" A woman peered in, a large covered tray balanced in her arms.

"Not at all! We're just finishing setup." Sarah hurried to help her with the door. "Perfect timing!"

"I'm Betty," she said with a smile. "I made my famous ginger molasses cookies. They're still slightly warm."

Margaret guided her toward the cookie tables. "Let me help you find a good spot for these," she said, leading Betty to a table with available space.

Within twenty minutes, the trickle of arrivals turned into a steady stream. People of all ages—from teenagers to grandparents—arrived with platters, tins, and decorative boxes filled with holiday cookies. Each had prepared dozens of a single variety, ready to exchange for an assortment of others.

Sarah greeted guests at the door while Margaret managed the check-in process, explaining the rules of the exchange.

"Once everyone has arrived and set up, we'll ring this bell," Margaret told a newcomer, pointing to an old-fashioned school bell on the counter. "Then you can take this empty container and make your way around the displays, taking one or two of each cookie you'd like to try. We ask that you follow the arrows for traffic flow."

By five o'clock, The Book Nook hummed with conversation and laughter. Holiday music played softly in the background as women circled the displays, admiring the cookies and exchanging baking tips.

"You absolutely must try Elaine's chocolate peppermint stars," one woman insisted to her friend. "She uses that special dark cocoa from a gourmet shop in Portland."

Another cluster gathered around a display of elaborately decorated sugar cookies shaped like snowflakes and Christmas trees, discussing royal icing techniques and the merits of various piping tips.

Sarah wove through the crowd, refilling napkin dispensers and making sure everyone had what they needed. She caught Margaret's eye across the room and mouthed a silent "thank you," receiving a thumbs-up in return.

Despite the crowd, the bookstore maintained its comfortable atmosphere. The cookie exchange had transformed it into a welcoming refuge from the December chill outside. Several attendees browsed the bookshelves between sampling cookies, and Sarah noticed with satisfaction that quite a few carried books they planned to purchase. Her impromptu hosting idea was turning out to be good for business as well.

"Sarah!" Margaret's urgent whisper caught her attention. "We're out of the gingerbread white hot chocolate already."

Sarah's eyes widened. "Already? I made double what I thought we'd need."

"It was too good," Margaret said. "Everyone's raving about it."

"There's more mix in the storage room," Sarah said. "Can you handle things here while I make another batch?"

"Absolutely. Go."

As Sarah disappeared into the back, Margaret continued to manage the flow of the event.

The bell above the door jingled again, and Margaret turned to see a flustered-looking woman rushing in, carrying a plastic container from the grocery store bakery.

"Am I too late?" the woman asked breathlessly. "My sister-in-law invited me at the last minute."

Margaret glanced at the obviously store-bought cookies, frosted in garish colors and stamped with generic holiday shapes. The woman's embarrassed expression told Margaret everything she needed to know.

"Not at all," Margaret said, keeping her voice low. "Let me help you get settled."

She quickly produced a blank recipe card and slid it across the table. "Just write 'Holiday Sugar Cookies,'" she suggested discreetly. "There's a spot left on the table by the window."

The woman's relief was evident. "Thank you. I tried to bake last night, but it was a disaster," she whispered. "I didn't want to come empty-handed."

"We've all been there," Margaret assured her. "The important thing is participating in the fun."

As the evening progressed, the cookie exchange hit its stride. Sarah returned with a fresh batch of her gingerbread white hot chocolate, receiving a round of spontaneous applause when she announced its arrival.

Just as things seemed to be running perfectly, a crash and

several gasps drew everyone's attention to a corner of the store. A small display of holiday books had toppled over when someone had reached too enthusiastically for a cookie platter.

"I'm so sorry!" A young woman crouched down, frantically gathering scattered books. "I didn't see them when I was reaching for the s'mores cookies."

Sarah hurried over, kneeling to help. "No harm done," she said, though Margaret could see her quickly assessing each book for damage. "These are just our regular stock, not the antiques."

Crisis averted, the exchange continued. Margaret overheard snippets of conversation as she circulated through the crowd, making sure everything ran smoothly.

"Did someone actually bring fruitcake cookies?" one woman asked, her nose wrinkled.

"I'm Lori, and those are mine," responded an elegant older woman. She stood tall, chin lifted slightly. "My grandmother's recipe, brought from Europe three generations ago."

"Well, I'm sorry, but fruitcake is simply inedible," the woman declared. "It's a universal truth."

"Perhaps you've never had proper fruitcake," Lori countered, reaching for the plate. "Try one."

A small crowd gathered, watching the exchange with amusement.

"I don't think I should waste my cookie allowance on—"

"Taste it," Lori insisted, her tone leaving no room for argument.

With obvious reluctance, the woman accepted a small cookie studded with colorful bits of dried fruit. She took a tiny bite, her expression skeptical. Then her eyebrows rose in surprise.

"That's... actually good," she admitted, sounding genuinely shocked. "What on earth is in these?"

"Homemade candied citrus peel soaked in brandy for three

months," Lori said triumphantly. "Not those horrifying neon cherries from the grocery store."

The crowd erupted in laughter, and several people reached for the suddenly popular fruitcake cookies.

"The Great Fruitcake Debate has been settled!" someone called out, prompting more laughter.

By seven o'clock, the crowd had thinned considerably. Women departed with containers full of assorted cookies, recipe cards tucked carefully inside. Many carried newly purchased books as well.

Sarah collapsed into a chair behind the counter, her smile tired but genuine. "I can't believe we pulled this off."

Margaret sat beside her, passing over a cup of the gingerbread white hot chocolate. "Not only pulled it off—it was a triumph. I overheard at least five people saying this was the best cookie exchange the town has ever had."

"Really?" Sarah's eyes brightened.

"Really. And I counted fourteen book sales that wouldn't have happened otherwise."

Sarah sighed with relief, taking a sip of her drink. "Thanks again, Margaret. I couldn't have done this without you."

"What are friends for?" Margaret replied, reaching for one of the few remaining cookies on a nearby plate. "Now, I think we've earned a sampling of our own, don't you?"

Sarah laughed and reached for a cookie. "Absolutely."

* * *

At the marina, Chris welcomed ten bundled-up customers onto the *Blue Heron* for the evening's Back Bay Christmas Lights Tour. Wind whistled through the dock, carrying the sharp bite of winter air as passengers hurried aboard, shoulders hunched against the cold.

"Welcome aboard," Chris greeted each person, trying to infuse enthusiasm into his voice to compensate for the decidedly unwarm conditions. "We'll be setting off in about five minutes."

The passengers filed into the cabin, their expressions falling as they entered the space. Chris had focused his decorating efforts on the exterior railings of the boat, stringing twinkling lights along the perimeter that looked charming from the shore. But inside, the cabin remained completely unadorned—just the standard seating and windows of his regular bird-watching tours. No festive lights, no decorations, nothing to transform the interior into the cozy holiday experience passengers had expected.

"Is there heating?" one woman asked, rubbing her gloved hands together.

"The engine provides some warmth," Chris explained, knowing full well it was inadequate for a December evening. "It'll warm up once we get moving."

This wasn't entirely true, but he hoped the excitement of seeing the decorated waterfront homes would distract from the temperature.

Chris took his position at the helm and started the engine. As the *Blue Heron* pulled away from the dock, he picked up the microphone for the boat's small PA system.

"Good evening, folks! I'm Chris, your captain for tonight's Back Bay Christmas Lights Tour. We'll be cruising past some of the most elaborately decorated waterfront properties in the area, with a brief stop halfway through at the marina pier for complimentary hot chocolate."

He adjusted the volume on the Christmas music that had been playing softly in the background, letting the holiday melodies fill the cabin space.

A few passengers nodded politely, but most were already huddling deeper into their coats, looking considerably less enthusiastic than when they'd boarded.

The boat picked up speed, cutting through the dark water. The icy wind seemed to find every seam in the cabin windows, creating a persistent cold draft. Chris had checked the weather forecast—thirty-eight degrees with moderate wind—manageable conditions for a boat tour, technically speaking.

"Coming up on our right is the Mathison house," Chris announced, pointing toward a waterfront home festooned with thousands of white lights and illuminated reindeer on the lawn. "They've won the local holiday decorating contest three years running."

A few passengers glanced in the direction he indicated, but their appreciation was muted. One elderly couple had pulled a shared scarf across both their laps like a makeshift blanket.

Chris continued his commentary as they cruised past more decorated homes, trying to maintain his enthusiasm despite the increasingly obvious discomfort of his passengers. A family with two teenagers had resorted to huddling together in a single row of seats, while a middle-aged woman kept checking her watch every few minutes.

Suddenly, the *Blue Heron* hit the wake of a larger vessel passing in the channel. The boat jerked roughly, causing several passengers to grab onto their seats.

"Sorry about that, folks," Chris called out. "Just a bit of—"

Before he could finish, a spray of freezing cold water shot through a small crack in one of the cabin windows, soaking the sleeve and side of a man in the front row and splashing onto two other nearby passengers.

"What the—" The man jumped up, frantically brushing at his soaked coat sleeve.

"I am so sorry," Chris said, immediately leaving the helm and grabbing the small stack of paper towels he kept for birdwatching equipment cleanup. "There must be a crack in the seal."

The affected passengers dabbed uselessly at their wet clothing with the flimsy paper towels. A woman with water spots on her wool coat pulled a scarf from her bag and tried to blot the damage.

"Is there any heat at all in this boat?" she asked, her voice sharp with frustration.

"The engine provides some ambient heat," Chris repeated, knowing how insufficient it sounded. "We'll be stopping for hot chocolate in about fifteen minutes."

He returned to the helm, his stomach tight with anxiety. This was not at all how he had envisioned his Christmas Lights Tour. The brochure had promised "a magical evening cruise viewing spectacular holiday light displays from the unique vantage point of Back Bay's waters." Instead, he was providing a cold, uncomfortable, and now wet experience for paying customers.

Chris attempted to salvage the tour, pointing out particularly impressive displays and sharing historical tidbits about the properties they passed. But few were listening now. Most passengers had retreated into resigned silence, clearly counting the minutes until they could return to shore.

The stop at the marina pier for hot chocolate provided brief respite, but even there, Chris could overhear murmured complaints as passengers gratefully wrapped cold hands around paper cups.

"Worst forty dollars I've spent this season," one man muttered to his wife.

"At least the hot chocolate is good," she replied charitably.

Back on the boat for the return journey, the atmosphere had turned from anticipatory to defeated. When they finally docked, the passengers hurried down the gangplank with barely a goodbye, faces pinched with cold and disappointment.

Chris caught up with the three who had been soaked by the window spray.

"I'd like to offer you a partial refund," he said, pulling out his wallet. "I'm very sorry about the window and the discomfort."

They accepted the twenty-dollar bills gratefully, though their expressions remained strained. No one mentioned returning for another tour or recommending the experience to friends.

Twenty minutes later, Chris sat in his truck in the now-empty parking lot, heat blasting, as he called Sarah. When she answered, he could hear the quiet sounds of cleanup in the background.

"Hey there," Sarah said. "How did tonight's tour go?"

"Absolute disaster," Chris replied, his voice flat. "I think I just delivered the worst Christmas experience in Back Bay history."

"Oh no!" Sarah's voice immediately filled with concern. "What happened?"

Chris leaned his head back against the headrest. "Everything. The boat was too cold. There was a crack in one of the windows that I didn't know about, and water sprayed in when we hit a wake. Three people got soaked. Everyone was miserable." He sighed deeply. "I had to give partial refunds to the people who got wet, and honestly, I should have refunded everyone."

"I'm so sorry," Sarah said. "That sounds awful."

"It was. You should have seen their faces, Sarah. They couldn't wait to get off the boat. I feel terrible."

"Is the window badly damaged?"

"No, it's just a small crack in the seal, but enough for water to spray through when hit at the right angle."

"That's fixable, right?" Sarah asked.

"Yeah, I could probably replace the seal tomorrow."

"Well, that's one problem solved," Sarah said practically. "What about the cold? Is there any way to add heating to the cabin?"

Chris considered this. "Not real heating. The electrical system isn't set up for it. But..." His thoughts started turning. "I could bring a stack of blankets for people to use during the trip. Maybe even some of those disposable hand warmers to give out when people board. And I should be more upfront about the heating situation when people book tickets so they know what to expect."

"That's a great idea," Sarah encouraged. "And what about atmosphere? You mentioned stringing lights outside the boat, but what about inside the cabin?"

"I didn't think about that," Chris admitted. "I focused on how the boat would look from shore, not how it would feel for the passengers."

"A few strands of battery-operated Christmas lights inside could transform the space," Sarah suggested. "And what about the music—is it creating the right mood?"

"I do play Christmas music," Chris said. "But it's just jazz instrumental covers—maybe I should use more upbeat Christmas tunes that people can actually recognize and sing along with."

"Exactly! Familiar Christmas songs would definitely help create that festive feeling you're going for."

As Sarah continued offering practical solutions, Chris felt his spirits gradually lifting. These were all simple, inexpensive changes that could transform the experience.

"You know what? You're right," he said, his voice strengthening. "I can fix this. The concept is still good—people want to see the lights from the water. I just need to make the experience more comfortable and festive."

"There you go," Sarah said with approval. "Every new business has setbacks. This is just a bump in the road."

"A pretty big bump," Chris said, but with a hint of humor returning to his voice.

"Nothing you can't handle," Sarah assured him.

Chris laughed for the first time that evening. "Fair point. How did the cookie exchange go?"

"I'll tell you all about it tomorrow. Right now, focus on getting warm and making your list of improvements. This isn't the end of your Christmas tour idea—it's just the beginning of making it better."

* * *

Darkness settled over the bay house as Nick adjusted the last of the three trail cameras they'd installed the day before. The small devices were strategically placed—one facing the deck, another monitoring the garage, and the third positioned to capture the side yard where the garden lights had disappeared.

"How's that?" Nick called over to Lisa, who was checking the camera angle on her phone through the wireless connection.

"Perfect," she replied, giving him a thumbs up. "If anyone so much as breathes near your property, we'll know about it."

Nick climbed down from the stepladder and dusted off his hands. "I still can't believe how many things have gone missing. I did a thorough check of everything I've brought over, and there's definitely more than what we noticed earlier."

Lisa looked up from her phone. "What else is missing?"

"My wool scarf—the blue one I bought last Christmas—I hung it on a hook by the back door last week when it got warm while I was working. And now I've noticed a small garden trowel is missing from my toolbox in the garage." Nick's face clouded with frustration. "I'm starting to question whether this neighborhood is as peaceful as I thought."

Lisa frowned, tucking her phone into her back pocket. "Maybe we should make a list of everything that's disappeared. If there's a pattern, it might tell us something about who's taking them."

"Good idea," Nick agreed, following her onto the deck, where they'd set up their makeshift surveillance headquarters. A small table held two thermoses of coffee, a box of donuts from the local bakery, and a notebook for recording any suspicious activity. "I'm really starting to have second thoughts about this place."

"Don't jump to conclusions yet," Lisa said, sitting down in one of the Adirondack chairs. She opened the notebook to a fresh page and wrote "Missing Items" at the top. "Let's see... the striped cushions, work gloves, and solar lights." She paused to write them down. "And now the wool scarf and garden trowel. Anything else?"

Nick shook his head, pacing the length of the deck. "Not that I've noticed, but I'm sure there are things I've forgotten about."

"Do you think it could be locals?" Lisa asked, tapping the pen against the notebook. "Maybe they're not thrilled about a newcomer buying the property?"

"That's what I've been wondering," Nick admitted, stopping to lean against the railing. "Maybe it's some kind of initiation—prank the new guy, see how he reacts. The real estate agent did mention this area has families that have lived here for generations."

Lisa added a note to the page. "Well, if it is a prank, it's not very funny. But it beats the alternative of having an actual thief targeting the house."

Nick stood up and stretched. "Speaking of which, let me get the fire pit going. It'll make our stakeout a bit cozier."

While Nick went down to the beach to light the fire, Lisa continued to stare out at the property, trying to make sense of the strange disappearances. She could see how much this place meant to him—the quietness, the sense of peace he'd found in making this his home. The thought that someone might be deliberately targeting his house made her worry about how it was affecting him.

"Fire's ready!" Nick called from below, interrupting her worried thoughts.

Lisa grabbed their supplies and joined him at the fire pit, where flames were already dancing among the stacked wood. The circle of stones glowed in the firelight, and the gentle lapping of waves provided a soothing soundtrack to their vigil.

"This is actually kind of nice," Lisa commented, pulling her chair closer to the fire. She poured coffee into two mugs and handed one to Nick. "Donuts and coffee by firelight. If it weren't for the potential thief, this would be a perfect evening."

Nick smiled, feeling some of his tension ease as he sat beside her. "You have a knack for finding the bright side of things."

"One of my many talents," she replied with a wink, pulling a blanket around her shoulders. "Along with my exceptional detective skills, of course."

"Of course," Nick agreed, taking a sip of his coffee. "Detective Lisa on the case."

They settled into a comfortable silence, broken only by the crackle of the fire and the distant call of a night bird. Every so often, one of them would scan the property with the small binoculars they'd brought, focusing on dark corners and the edges of the tree line.

Hours passed with no sign of activity. They talked intermittently, their conversation flowing easily from theories about the thief to plans for the house to stories from their past. Around eleven, Lisa pulled out the second thermos of coffee to warm them up.

"To keep us alert," she explained, pouring the rich liquid into their mugs. "The night is still young."

By midnight, however, Nick's energy had faded. His head drooped forward, then jerked back up several times before he finally surrendered to sleep, his breathing becoming deep and even.

Lisa smiled fondly at him but remained vigilant. She added another log to the fire and continued her watch, occasionally checking the trail camera app on her phone. No alerts had come through yet.

The night grew cooler, and Lisa pulled her blanket tighter around her shoulders. The fire cast long shadows that seemed to dance and shift with each flicker of the flames. She found herself staring into the darkness beyond the circle of light, where the yard met the trees at the property's edge.

A rustling sound caught her attention—subtle at first, like leaves shifting in a breeze, but there was no wind tonight. Lisa squinted, trying to penetrate the darkness. The sound came again, more distinct this time, from the cluster of trees to the left of the yard.

Lisa leaned forward, straining to see. For a moment, there was nothing but silence and shadows. Then, suddenly, two glowing eyes appeared in the darkness, staring directly at her.

Lisa screamed, the sound piercing the quiet night. Nick jerked awake, nearly falling out of his chair.

"What? What is it?" he asked frantically, looking around.

"There! In the trees!" Lisa gasped, already on her feet. "Someone's watching us!"

Nick jumped up, knocking over his empty mug. Without hesitation, they both dashed across the beach and up the stairs to the deck, hearts pounding. They burst through the back door, slamming it shut behind them and turning the deadbolt with trembling fingers.

"What did you see?" Nick demanded, peering through the curtains at the abandoned fire pit below.

Lisa pressed a hand to her chest, trying to catch her breath. "I'm not sure. There was a noise in the trees, and then... eyes. Two eyes, glowing in the dark, staring right at me."

"A person?" Nick asked, his voice tense.

"I don't know," Lisa admitted, joining him at the window. "It was too dark to make out a shape. But whatever it was, it was watching us. I'm certain of it."

They stood side by side, peering nervously through the gap in the curtains at the shadowy yard below. The fire still burned in the pit, casting an eerie glow over the empty chairs they'd abandoned.

Nick pulled out his phone and checked the trail camera app. "Nothing," he said, his brow furrowed in confusion. "Not a single alert from any of the cameras."

Lisa looked at him, bewilderment in her eyes. "How is that possible? I know I saw something out there."

Nick shook his head slowly, the mystery deepening with each passing moment. "I don't know," he admitted, his gaze returning to the darkness beyond the window. "But something strange is happening at this house, and I'm starting to think it might be more than just a neighborhood prank."

CHAPTER EIGHT

Margaret sank deeper into the plush cushions of their farmhouse sofa, propping her feet on the coffee table as Dave handed her a mug of hot chocolate topped with a generous swirl of whipped cream. The house was quiet except for the gentle crackle of the fireplace and the occasional whistling of the wind against the windows.

"So we're decided then?" Dave asked, settling beside her. "Christmas at the beach house?"

Margaret nodded, taking a sip of her cocoa. "Absolutely. The girls are excited about it, and I love the idea of waking up Christmas morning with the ocean just a few blocks away."

"I can already picture it," Dave said, stretching his arm along the back of the sofa. "Christmas morning coffee on the porch, stockings on the new mantel..."

"Actually," Margaret said, shifting to face him. "I've been thinking—what if we hosted an open house on Christmas Eve?"

Dave raised his eyebrows. "An open house?"

"A Christmas Eve buffet," Margaret continued, warming to the idea as she spoke. "Something casual where friends and family could drop by throughout the evening. No formal sit-down dinner, just good food and company. People could come and go as they please."

Dave considered this for a moment then smiled. "I love that idea. Who would we invite?"

"Anyone who wants to come, really. Family and friends. The neighbors from here and the beach house. Even Tom and Nanette Wilson, if they'd like to join us." Margaret took another sip of her hot chocolate. "I just love the idea of making the beach house a gathering place right from the start."

"A new Christmas memory," Dave said, nodding slowly. "The beach house becoming a place of community, not just a private retreat."

"Exactly." Margaret set her mug on a coaster and reached for the notepad she kept on the side table. "We could do a nice buffet spread, nothing too fussy. Maybe some shrimp or crab cakes—being so close to the ocean. A charcuterie board. And a spiral ham that people can make little sandwiches from."

Dave leaned over to look at her list. "Don't forget your sugar cookies. And we should definitely have that spiced wine punch you made last year."

"And plenty of non-alcoholic options too," Margaret added, jotting down ideas. "Hot chocolate for the kids, sparkling cider..."

"We could string some extra lights on the porch," Dave suggested, his enthusiasm building. "Make it look inviting from the street. Maybe put luminaries along the walkway."

They continued planning, tossing ideas back and forth with growing excitement. The beach house renovation had been completed just in time for the holidays, and hosting an open house felt like the perfect way to christen their new space.

Margaret was in the middle of describing her vision for the dining table arrangement when a raised voice drifted through the air from somewhere outside. They both paused, listening.

"Did you hear that?" Dave asked, setting down his mug.

Margaret nodded, already rising from the sofa. "It sounded like someone shouting. From the direction of the Wilson farm."

They moved to the kitchen window that faced the woods. In the dim evening light, they couldn't see anything unusual, but another angry exclamation drifted toward them, the words indistinct but the tone unmistakable.

"Something's wrong," Margaret said, reaching for her coat on the hook by the back door. "We should check on Tom and Nanette."

Dave nodded, grabbing his own jacket. "Agreed."

They hurried across their backyard and into the woods, following the now-familiar path that led to the Christmas tree farm. As they drew closer, the voices became clearer, and Margaret could make out Tom Wilson's distinctive baritone, sharper than she'd ever heard it.

"I told you once, and I'm telling you again," Tom's voice rang out. "This property is not for sale at that price. Not now, not ever."

"One million isn't enough for you?" demanded another male voice, unfamiliar and cutting. "That's nearly twice what this land is worth on the market, Mr. Wilson. You're being unreasonable."

Dave and Margaret exchanged a glance as they quickened their pace through the last stretch of woods. They emerged at the edge of the tree farm to see Tom standing in his driveway, facing a man in an expensive-looking gray suit. The stranger held an open folder of documents, which he jabbed at periodically to emphasize his points.

Tom's face was flushed with anger. "I didn't invite you here today. You showing up unannounced isn't going to change my mind."

"Your property taxes are only going to increase," the suited man—Mitchell—argued, his voice smooth despite the evident frustration. "And maintaining this place is clearly becoming too much for someone your age. Be practical, Mr. Wilson."

Before Tom could respond, the cabin door swung open, and Nanette emerged onto the porch, still wearing a baking apron, her eyes flashing with fury.

"Practical?" she repeated, her normally gentle voice sharp. "This land has been in our family for generations. It belonged to Tom's parents, and his grandparents, and his great-grandparents before that. Don't lecture us about being practical."

Mitchell sighed dramatically. "Mrs. Wilson, I understand sentimentality, but—"

"I don't think you do," Dave interrupted as he and Margaret approached, making their presence known.

Mitchell turned, startled by the new voices. His expression quickly shifted from annoyance to a smoothly professional smile. "And you are?"

"Dave and Margaret," Dave said, stepping forward to stand beside Tom. "Neighbors and friends of the Wilsons."

"Ah," Mitchell said, closing his folder with a practiced movement. "Well, this is a private business matter between myself and the Wilsons."

"A private matter that you're conducting by showing up unannounced and raising your voice?" Margaret asked, moving to stand near Nanette on the porch steps.

Mitchell's smile tightened. "As I was explaining to Mr. Wilson, my company is prepared to make a very generous offer for this property."

"Which we've already declined," Tom said firmly. "Twice now."

Dave rested a hand lightly on Tom's shoulder. "I think the Wilsons have made their position clear. Perhaps you should come back another time. By invitation only."

Mitchell looked from Dave to Tom to Nanette, and finally to Margaret, assessing the unified front they presented. After a moment, he tucked the folder under his arm with a slight shrug.

"Very well. But my offer won't stay on the table forever, Mr.

Wilson. The market fluctuates, and so do opportunities." He reached into his breast pocket and extracted a business card, which he extended toward Tom. "When you're ready to discuss this rationally, give me a call."

Tom made no move to take the card, so Mitchell placed it on the hood of Tom's pickup truck. He nodded curtly to the group then walked toward a black luxury sedan parked on the dirt road.

"I'll be in touch," he called over his shoulder. "With an even better offer."

They watched in silence as Mitchell's car pulled away, dust rising from the dirt road in its wake. Once it was out of sight, Tom let out a long breath, his shoulders slumping slightly.

"Thank you both," he said, looking between Dave and Margaret. "That fellow's been a persistent thorn in my side for weeks now."

"Are you okay?" Margaret asked, noticing how Tom's hands were trembling.

"Oh, I'm fine," Tom said, though the weariness in his voice suggested otherwise. "Just tired of having the same conversation over and over."

Nanette came down the porch steps and took her husband's arm. "That man has no respect for boundaries or for our family's history with this land."

"High Tide Development," Dave said, picking up the business card from the truck hood and reading it. "I've heard of them. They build those cookie-cutter subdivisions all over the county."

Tom nodded grimly. "That's what he wants to do here. Clear-cut the entire property and put up forty-some houses. Called it 'progress.'"

"That's terrible," Margaret said, looking out at the beautiful rows of evergreens stretching into the distance.

"Anyway," Tom said, clearly wanting to change the subject,

"what brings you two over this evening? Something we can help you with?"

Margaret glanced at Dave before responding. "We heard voices and wanted to make sure everything was okay. But actually, we were just talking about getting ready for Christmas."

"Oh?" Nanette brightened at this. "Are you planning something special?"

"We are," Margaret said. "We're going to spend Christmas at our beach house in town, and we're hosting an open house on Christmas Eve. We'd love for you both to come, if you're not too busy with the farm."

"That's very kind," Tom said, his expression warming. "Christmas Eve is typically our last busy day for tree sales, but things usually wind down by late afternoon. We do have family plans later in the evening, but we'd love to stop by for a bit if that works."

"That sounds perfect," Dave said. "Even if you can only stay for a little while, we'd love to have you." He glanced around at the farm. "You know, we'd be happy to help out this evening if you have customers coming. Might take your mind off that unpleasant encounter."

Tom looked surprised by the offer. "You sure? It's your evening too, you know."

"We'd love to," Margaret insisted. "We had such a good time helping the other night."

Tom and Nanette exchanged a glance, silent communication passing between them before Tom nodded. "Well, if you're offering, we won't turn you down. We've got a few families scheduled to come by in about half an hour to pick out their trees."

"I just made a caramel apple pie," Nanette added. "It's cooling in the kitchen. Why don't you both come inside for a minute while we wait for customers to arrive?"

As they followed the Wilsons toward the cabin, Margaret noticed Tom walking stiffly, favoring his knees more than usual.

The confrontation with Mitchell had taken a visible toll on him.

Once inside, Nanette busied herself with making coffee while Tom gestured for Dave and Margaret to take seats at the kitchen table. He lowered himself into a chair with a slight grimace.

"Those developer types," he said, shaking his head. "They see land and all they think about is how to divide it up and cover it with pavement and houses."

"It must be difficult," Margaret said sympathetically. "Having to keep turning them away."

Tom nodded, absently tracing a whorl in the wooden tabletop with his finger. "The money they're offering—it's substantial. More than the property is worth by traditional measures. But how do you put a price on something like this?" He gestured toward the window, where the rows of evergreens were visible in the fading light.

"You can't," Dave said simply.

"No, you can't," Tom agreed. He looked up at them, his blue eyes sharp despite his apparent fatigue. "You two ever think about buying land? This place would suit you."

The question hung in the air for a moment. Margaret caught Dave's eye across the table, seeing her own surprise reflected there, along with something else—a spark of interest, perhaps even excitement.

Before either of them could respond, the sound of a car engine drifted in from outside, followed by children's voices raised in excitement. Tom pushed himself to his feet with a small grunt.

"First customers of the evening," he announced. "Let's get to work."

"Actually," Margaret said, glancing at her watch, "I should run home first to get the girls. They're due back from my parents any minute, and they wanted to help out this time."

Dave caught her eye briefly, a silent acknowledgment of the

question that now hovered between them, unaddressed but impossible to ignore. "I'll stay and help Tom until you get back with Harper and Abby," he said.

* * *

The front door of Donna's Restaurant swung open, letting in a blast of cold air along with a family of five, their cheeks rosy from the winter evening and the excitement of the Christmas carnival. Dale watched from his position near the hostess stand as Julia, their newest server, led them to one of the last available tables, expertly navigating the crowded dining room with menus in hand.

The restaurant was packed, every table filled and a small line forming at the entrance. The steady thrum of conversation and laughter nearly drowned out the Christmas music from the carnival outside, and the air was rich with the aromas of their new carnival-inspired dishes.

Dale caught sight of a server emerging from the kitchen, balancing a tray loaded with their gourmet fried Oreos drizzled with caramel and paired with housemade vanilla bean ice cream. At the table where they were delivered, a young girl's eyes widened with delight.

"Twenty-minute wait for a table of four," Julia called to Dale as she passed by with a tray of their upscale corn dogs made with housemade sausage. "Should I tell them?"

Dale glanced at his watch. "Yes, but offer them hot chocolate while they wait. The salted caramel one."

He made his way through the dining room, stopping occasionally to check on tables or assist a server. The transformation of their business in just a few days had been remarkable. What had started as a desperate attempt to salvage their busy holiday week had turned into an unexpected windfall. Their carnival-inspired menu, initially conceived as a compromise, had become a sensation.

Through the front windows, Dale could see Donna at her funnel cake cart, positioned strategically near the entrance to the carnival. Even from here, he could tell she was in her element—laughing with customers, dusting powdered sugar with a flourish, and somehow managing to look completely unfazed by the line that stretched halfway down the block. She had set up a small sign advertising the restaurant's carnival menu, and from what Dale could see, many people in line were reading it with interest.

His phone buzzed with a text from Donna: "Need more batter ASAP! And extra sugar!"

Dale made a mental note to send someone out with supplies, then pushed through the swinging doors into the kitchen. The scene that greeted him was controlled chaos—line cooks working at full capacity, the dish station running nonstop, and tickets continuing to print at an alarming rate.

"How are we looking on the special corn dogs and BBQ sliders?" Dale asked, moving to the expediting station.

"Fifteen corn dogs ready now, twenty more prepped," replied Pete, their head line cook, without looking up from the sauté station where he was working on three orders simultaneously. "And we've got six BBQ sliders on the grill right now."

"And the hot chocolate bar?"

"We're keeping up, but barely," answered Tanya, who was responsible for desserts and beverages. "The peppermint one is the most popular. We might run out by nine if it keeps up like this."

Dale checked the clock on the wall—it was already seven-fifteen. "I'll ask Antonio to prep another batch. And let's make sure we're ready for the post-ride crowd when the carnival starts winding down after ten."

Their extended hours had been another success, catching the hungry carnival-goers after the rides closed. Last night, they'd served nearly fifty tables between ten and midnight, a time when they would normally be closed.

The takeout window—another of Donna's impromptu ideas—had been converted from an unused service entrance. It now had a constant stream of customers ordering their gourmet hot chocolate, specialty sandwiches, and other portable versions of their carnival-inspired menu items.

"Dale," called Eduardo, their assistant manager, from across the kitchen. "We're running low on the honey mustard aioli for the corn dogs. Should I have the cooks start on another batch?"

Dale nodded, checking the ticket times. "Yes, and see if we can speed up the current orders. Table twelve has been waiting seventeen minutes."

For the next hour, Dale moved through the kitchen like a conductor, coordinating the various stations, helping where needed, and ensuring that every dish met their standards before it left the kitchen. Despite the frantic pace, there was an undeniable energy in the air—a kind of collective exhilaration that came from successfully rising to a challenge.

The staff, though visibly exhausted, seemed to be riding the same wave of adrenaline. Even Todd, one of their line cooks who had initially complained the most about the extended hours, was now moving with purpose between tasks, a faint smile on his face as he called out completed orders.

Around eight-thirty, Dale felt a hand on his shoulder and turned to find Donna, her cheeks flushed from the cold outside and a light dusting of powdered sugar on her jacket.

"I've left Mia in charge of the cart for a bit," she said, her eyes bright with excitement. "Funnel cakes are selling faster than we can make them. We've already gone through twice as much batter as yesterday."

Dale couldn't help but smile at her enthusiasm. "Same story in here. Every table's full, and we've got a waiting list."

Donna looked around the kitchen, taking in the controlled frenzy with obvious satisfaction. "You know what we should do? Take a break. Go experience the carnival ourselves for an hour."

Dale raised an eyebrow. "Now? In the middle of our busiest dinner service in months?"

"Yes, now," Donna insisted. "The team has this under control. And we should see what all the fuss is about. It's been three days, and we haven't even ridden the Ferris wheel yet. Plus they'll call if they need us."

Dale hesitated, surveying the kitchen in full swing. It was true that they had a capable staff, and with Eduardo managing and Pete, Antonio, and Todd on the line, the kitchen was in good hands. Still, leaving during a rush went against every instinct he'd developed over years in the restaurant business.

"I don't know, Donna. The next wave of takeout orders will start soon, and—"

"I've got it covered," interrupted Eduardo, who had overheard their conversation. "Antonio and Todd are handling the line, I'll expedite, and Julia and the front of house team have everything under control. Go. An hour. You've both been working nonstop since this carnival arrived."

Dale looked from Eduardo to Donna, who was already removing her chef's coat to reveal a red sweater underneath.

"And you'll call if anything—"

"We've got this," Eduardo assured him, practically shooing them toward the exit. "Go have fun."

Minutes later, Dale found himself standing in the middle of the Christmas carnival, surrounded by twinkling lights, the sounds of laughter and excited screams from the rides, and the pervasive scent of kettle corn and cinnamon. The night air was cold but not unbearable, and Donna had linked her arm through his as they strolled past game booths where carnival barkers called out to passersby.

"Isn't this something?" Donna said, looking around with childlike wonder. "I haven't been to a carnival since I was a teenager."

Dale had to admit that the scene was impressive. The carnival company had transformed the ordinary parking lot into a winter wonderland. Colorful lights were strung between poles, casting a cheerful glow over everything. The rides—a Ferris wheel, a carousel, a small roller coaster, and several other attractions clearly designed for families—were all adorned with Christmas decorations. The game booths featured holiday themes, and the workers wore Santa hats or elf costumes.

As they walked, Dale began to see the carnival through new eyes. What had first appeared to him as a noisy intrusion now seemed like a joyful celebration. Children ran from ride to ride, their faces lit with delight. Parents waited patiently, many of them holding cups of hot chocolate—some from the carnival vendors, but many, Dale noticed with satisfaction, from their own restaurant.

"I'll admit it," Dale said as they paused to watch a group of teenagers try their luck at a ring toss game. "This carnival has been good for business. Better than good, actually. If we keep up this pace, we might have our best December ever."

Donna squeezed his arm. "And it's not just about the money. The carnival has brought so much joy to people. You can see it in their faces."

They continued walking, pausing occasionally to admire a particularly elaborate Christmas display or to watch the carnival games. The music, which had initially driven Dale to distraction, now seemed to blend pleasantly with the overall atmosphere.

Suddenly, Donna stopped, pointing upward. "Look."

Dale followed her gaze to the Ferris wheel, its outline silhouetted against the night sky, hundreds of white lights tracing its circumference like stars that had been captured and arranged in a perfect circle.

"When's the last time we did something just for fun?" Donna asked, looking at him with a slight challenge in her eyes.

Dale considered the question. Between running the restaurant, planning menus, managing staff, and handling the business side of things, "fun" had often been postponed to some distant future date when they wouldn't be quite so busy—a date that somehow never arrived.

"Too long," he admitted.

"Then let's ride the Ferris wheel," Donna said, already pulling him toward the line. "Right now."

The line moved quickly, and soon they were being ushered into one of the small cars. The attendant lowered the safety bar, and with a slight jerk, they began to ascend. Donna immediately snuggled closer to Dale, partly for warmth and partly from excitement.

"I can't remember the last time I was on a Ferris wheel," she confessed as they rose higher.

As their car climbed higher, Cape May spread out below them in a tapestry of lights. The Victorian homes with their intricate gingerbread trim were outlined in white lights, while trees wrapped in multicolored strands created bursts of color throughout the area. Street lamps cast pools of golden light on the sidewalks, where people moved like miniature figures in a Christmas village display.

From this height, they could see all the way to the ocean, a dark expanse beyond the twinkling town, its presence felt rather than seen. The Washington Street Mall was particularly striking, transformed into a corridor of light that cut through the center of town.

Their car paused at the very top of the wheel, suspended for a moment between earth and sky. Dale felt a sense of perspective settle over him—not just of the town laid out below, but of his own recent attitudes and concerns.

"You were right," he said quietly. "About the carnival. About adapting instead of fighting it."

Donna smiled, her face illuminated by the carnival lights

below. "I wasn't completely sure myself. I just knew we had to try something different."

"It's been more than good for business," Dale continued. "It's been good for us too. I'd gotten stuck in a rut, thinking our restaurant could only be one thing. You saw the opportunity to evolve, even if just temporarily."

The Ferris wheel remained paused at the top, giving them a lingering view of Cape May adorned for the holidays.

As they sat snuggled together, the Ferris wheel began its descent, bringing them back toward the lively carnival below. But for that suspended moment high above Cape May, with the twinkling lights spread out beneath them like a reflection of the star-filled sky above, everything else faded away. The restaurant, the busy season, the day-to-day concerns—all of it disappeared, leaving only the two of them and the perfect clarity of the winter night.

CHAPTER NINE

Liz wrapped her hands around a steaming mug of coffee, savoring the quiet before the boys woke up. It had been a handful of days since she and Greg decided to put Furnish & Feast on hold for the holidays, and she was surprised by how much lighter she felt without the constant pressure of deadlines and deliveries.

"Sleep well?" Greg asked, shuffling into the kitchen in his robe and slippers.

"Better than I have in weeks," Liz replied, pouring him a cup of coffee and handing it to him.

Greg chuckled, accepting the mug gratefully. "I was thinking we could actually do some Christmas shopping today. You know, like normal people who aren't opening a restaurant in the coming year."

"What a novel concept," Liz said with a smile. "Shopping without calculating square footage or comparing furniture suppliers."

They were discussing their plans for the day when Greg's phone rang on the counter. He glanced at the screen and paused.

"Unknown number," he said, hesitating before answering. "Hello?"

Liz watched as Greg's expression shifted from relaxed to alert. He sat up straighter, pulling away from her slightly.

"Yes, this is Greg," he said. "Furnish and Feast, yes. What's that now?"

Liz set her mug down, suddenly attentive.

"When were they delivered? Just now?" Greg checked his watch. "And they're just sitting—I see. Yes, thank you for calling. We'll be right there."

He ended the call and turned to Liz, all traces of relaxation gone from his face. "That was Ron from the barbershop next door to Furnish & Feast. He says there are 'a ton of pallets' sitting out front of our store."

"What? At this hour?" Liz was already on her feet. "But we're not expecting any deliveries until after the holidays."

"Apparently someone didn't get that memo," Greg said, already heading for the stairs. "Ron said he noticed them when he was opening up this morning. He was worried they'd get stolen if left outside all day."

Liz followed him upstairs, her mind racing. "But we're not expecting anything until after the holidays. What could it be?"

"Let's just get over there first and see what we're dealing with," Greg suggested, pulling a sweater over his head.

Ten minutes later, they were dressed and heading out the door. Liz left a note for the boys explaining their sudden departure, though she doubted they'd emerge from their rooms before noon.

The drive to Furnish & Feast was quiet, both of them curious about what they might find as they navigated the morning streets.

"It's strange," Liz said, breaking the silence. "How does someone just drop off pallets without getting a signature or calling first?"

"That's what I'm wondering too," Greg replied. "Most

delivery companies won't leave anything that valuable unattended."

Frost had settled on the shop windows overnight, giving the downtown a sleepy, wintry look.

"There," Greg said as they turned onto their street. Even from half a block away, they could see the distinctive shapes of pallets and boxes stacked on the sidewalk in front of their store.

Greg parked hastily, and they hurried toward the building. As they approached, Liz's initial alarm gave way to confusion. The pallets were neatly arranged, completely shrink-wrapped, and accompanied by what appeared to be official delivery documentation.

Her eyes widened as she read. "Greg, these are from our supplier. The one that's supposed to be closed until January."

Greg was examining another slip. "This can't be right. This says 'café tables and chairs, wood/metal, standard height.'"

"And this one says 'home décor collection, spring/summer,'" Liz added, moving to another pallet. "These are all the things we actually ordered."

They exchanged bewildered glances.

"We should get these inside," Greg said, glancing up and down the street. "Before someone decides to help themselves to our inventory."

Liz nodded, and they set to work, using Greg's key to open the front door and beginning the process of moving everything inside. It took nearly two hours to transfer all the pallets and boxes from the sidewalk into the shop, both of them growing increasingly sweaty despite the winter chill.

Once everything was safely inside, Greg locked the door behind them and turned on the lights. The shop floor was now filled with new deliveries, separate from the children's furniture and party supplies they'd already set aside.

"I don't understand," Liz said, catching her breath. "Their customer service told you they were closed for the holidays."

Greg was examining one of the packing slips more carefully. "Look at this," he said, pointing to a handwritten note at the bottom. "It says 'Special delivery per management approval. See enclosed letter.'"

They began searching through the boxes until Liz found a sealed envelope taped to one of the pallets. She tore it open and unfolded the letter inside.

"'Dear Greg,'" she read aloud. "'Please accept our sincere apologies for the confusion with your recent orders. Upon investigation, we discovered a system error that resulted in your merchandise being misdirected. As a gesture of goodwill, we have expedited the delivery of your correct orders and included several additional items at no charge. We will arrange pickup of the incorrect items at your convenience after the holidays. We value your business and hope this resolves the matter to your satisfaction. Wishing you happy holidays and a successful opening for Furnish & Feast. Sincerely, Janet Brogan, CEO.'"

Greg looked around at the pallets surrounding them. "I guess someone at the supplier felt bad enough to make an exception to their holiday closure."

Liz was already cutting open the shrink wrap on one of the pallets. "Let's see what we've got."

The more they unwrapped and unpacked, the more excited they became. Each pallet and box revealed exactly what they had originally ordered—beautiful café tables with solid wood tops and black metal bases, comfortable yet stylish chairs to match, and all the home décor items Liz had carefully selected for her retail displays.

Greg assembled one of the café tables and set a chair beside it, then sat down with a satisfied smile. "Now this is more like it," he said, running his hand over the smooth surface of the table. "The perfect height for actual adults."

Liz was busy unpacking boxes of glass vases, rustic wood picture frames, seasonal decorations, silk flowers in vibrant colors, and ribbons in various prints and patterns. "These are exactly what I wanted," she said, arranging a few pieces on one of her restored sideboards. The accessories brought life to the space, making her furniture displays look complete and ready for customers.

"Look at this," Greg called from another pallet. "They sent us those pendant lights we couldn't afford. And there's an extra set of shelving units here."

Liz joined him, examining the bonus items. "Wow, they really went above and beyond. I'd say they more than made up for the mix-up."

For the next hour, they unpacked and arranged, periodically stopping to admire how the space was transforming. Greg set up several café tables in their designated area, while Liz created display vignettes throughout her section of the store. With each item they unpacked, Furnish & Feast came closer to matching the vision they'd held for so long.

"We should take some photos," Liz suggested, pulling out her phone. "To document the progress."

They took turns capturing images of the space—Greg's café area with its rustic tables and sleek chairs, Liz's furniture displays enhanced by carefully chosen accessories.

"It's really coming together," Greg said, looking around the transformed space. "I can actually see it now. Our shop."

Liz nodded, a lump forming in her throat. After weeks of setbacks and frustrations, seeing their vision taking physical form was overwhelming.

"We could keep working," Greg suggested, glancing at his watch. "Start unpacking more, maybe even assemble some of the additional shelving."

Liz was tempted. The momentum felt good, and the sight of their store finally looking like their plans was intoxicating. But then she remembered how they'd felt just days ago— exhausted, overwhelmed, pushed to their limits.

"Let's stick to the plan," she said firmly. "This will all be here in January. We're still on vacation."

Greg looked at her for a long moment then nodded. "You're right. We have plenty of time to get this right."

* * *

The street was bustling with holiday activity as Judy and Bob pulled into the parking lot of Charlotte's Way Inn. Christmas lights adorned the building's exterior, their cheerful brightness creating a welcoming beacon against the clear starlit sky.

"We're early," Bob noted, checking his watch as he turned off the engine.

"That was the plan," Judy reminded him, adjusting her scarf. "Henry said the good tables go quickly on karaoke nights."

They made their way inside, greeted by the familiar charm and festive atmosphere. The restaurant buzzed with anticipation tonight, conversations livelier than usual as diners seemed to be looking forward to the evening's entertainment.

"Look," Judy said, nudging Bob gently. "Henry's already here."

Sure enough, Henry sat at a table near the performance area. When he caught sight of them, his face brightened and he waved enthusiastically, gesturing to the two empty chairs he'd been saving.

"You came!" Henry exclaimed as they approached. He clasped Bob's hand then Judy's. "I was hoping you'd make it tonight."

"We couldn't resist," Bob replied, helping Judy with her coat before removing his own.

They settled into their seats, and a server promptly appeared to take their drink orders. The restaurant was filling up quickly, with diners claiming the best spots for viewing the evening's performances.

"Have you looked at the song list?" Henry asked after the server departed.

Judy and Bob exchanged glances. "Actually," Judy began, her voice slightly hesitant, "we were hoping you might help us choose something. We've been practicing a little, but we're still not entirely sure..."

Henry's face lit up. "You're going to sing? Both of you?"

"If we don't lose our nerve," Bob said with a smile.

"This is wonderful!" Henry reached down beside his chair and produced a shopping bag. "I brought these just in case you might be willing to give it a try." He reached into the bag and pulled out three Santa hats, each with a fluffy white trim and a small jingle bell at the tip. "Every performance needs the right costume."

Judy laughed as Henry placed one of the hats on his own head, the bell jingling with the movement. He offered the others to them with such earnest enthusiasm that Judy immediately took hers and put it on. Bob hesitated only briefly before following suit.

"Perfect," Henry declared, his eyes crinkling with delight. "Now, let's talk songs."

He produced a folded paper from his pocket—a printout of the karaoke selections. "I've marked a few that might suit your voices. Nothing too challenging for first-timers."

They leaned in together, reviewing the options. Henry pointed to several highlighted titles, occasionally humming a few notes to remind them of the melody.

"This one," Bob said suddenly, tapping the paper. "I've always liked this one."

Judy looked at his selection and smiled. "Really? I never knew that."

"Some things a man keeps to himself," Bob replied with mock seriousness. "Until karaoke night, apparently."

The hostess approached the microphone, welcoming everyone to the Christmas Karaoke Night. The first volunteer was a young woman whose rendition of "Last Christmas" earned appreciative applause. She was followed by a father-daughter duo performing a sweet, if slightly off-key, version of "Rudolph the Red-Nosed Reindeer."

"I should go up soon," Henry said, checking the sign-up list near their table. "I put my name down when I arrived."

"What will you sing tonight?" Judy asked.

"I think 'Silver Bells,'" Henry replied. "It always reminds me of the city at Christmas when Teresa and I were young."

When the hostess called Henry's name, several regular patrons perked up, turning their attention to the performance area. Henry rose, straightening his blazer and adjusting his Santa hat.

"Wish me luck," he said with a wink, though they all knew he needed no such thing.

As Henry took his position at the microphone, the restaurant grew noticeably quieter. His reputation had clearly spread since their last visit. When the music began, he closed his eyes briefly, then opened them to connect with the audience as he sang. His posture straightened as he swayed gently with the melody, every movement revealing his years of professional experience. Judy noticed diners at nearby tables pausing their conversations, silverware resting midair as they turned to watch.

When he finished, the applause was immediate and enthusiastic. Henry acknowledged it with a humble nod before making his way back to their table.

"Beautiful as always," Judy said as he sat down.

"Thank you, Judy," Henry replied, then leaned forward with an expectant smile. "And now, I believe it's your turn."

Judy felt a flutter of nervousness in her stomach. "Maybe we should wait a bit longer."

"No time like the present," Henry encouraged. "The crowd is warmed up, and you're as ready as you'll ever be."

Bob looked at Judy, raising an eyebrow in silent question. After a moment's hesitation, she nodded.

"Alright," Bob said, rising from his chair and offering Judy his hand. "Let's do this before I come to my senses."

They walked to the sign-up table, where the hostess smiled brightly at them. "First-timers?" she asked, noting their names.

"Is it that obvious?" Bob asked dryly.

"The Santa hats are a nice touch," she replied with a wink. "You'll be up after the next performer."

They returned to the table, where Henry gave them an encouraging thumbs-up. The current singer was a young man whose exuberant version of "Feliz Navidad" had several patrons clapping along.

"Remember," Henry said as the song concluded, "just enjoy yourselves. That's what matters most."

When the hostess called their names, Judy felt a moment of panic. Bob squeezed her hand reassuringly as they made their way to the front.

"We can still back out," he whispered.

"Not on your life," Judy replied, surprising herself with the determination in her voice.

They stood before the microphone, adjusting their Santa hats. The hostess helped them find their selection, and the opening notes of "Winter Wonderland" filled the restaurant.

Bob began, his voice quiet and slightly unsteady on the first line. Judy joined him for the second, and gradually, they found their rhythm together. Their voices weren't remarkable individually, but they complemented each other in a way that spoke of decades of harmony in all things.

As they reached the second verse, their nerves evident in their slightly wavering voices, Henry appeared beside them, apparently deciding to make good on his earlier offer. He added his rich baritone to their melody, and the welcome addition gave them both a boost of confidence, with Judy finding herself smiling as they continued.

Then, to her complete astonishment, Bob released her

hand and executed a perfect spin move. Judy responded, twirling gracefully under his arm before returning to position.

The spontaneous dance move delighted the audience, who responded with applause mid-song. Emboldened, Bob added a few more simple steps as they continued singing, transforming their performance into something more than they'd planned—a joyful celebration of music and movement.

When the final notes played, the restaurant erupted in cheers and applause far more enthusiastic than Judy had anticipated. She felt her cheeks flush with pleasure as Bob gave an exaggerated bow, tugging her into a small curtsy beside him.

"That was wonderful!" Henry exclaimed as they returned to the table, both slightly breathless from the experience.

"I can't believe we just did that," Judy said, laughing as she sat down. "And I certainly can't believe you knew those dance moves, Bob!"

"I'm surprised too," Bob admitted, his eyes bright with exhilaration. "They just sort of happened."

The manager of the restaurant approached their table, carrying a tray with three glasses of champagne. "Compliments of the house," he said, setting the glasses before them.

"Thank you," Judy replied, surprised by the gesture. "That was so much fun."

"Sometimes that's exactly what people need," the manager said with a smile before returning to his duties.

Throughout the remainder of the evening, patrons stopped by their table to offer compliments and share their own stories. An elderly woman told them about singing with her late husband in a church choir. A middle-aged couple confessed they'd been inspired to try karaoke themselves after watching the three of them.

"You've made quite an impression," Henry observed, raising his glass in a toast. "To new traditions."

"To new traditions," Judy and Bob echoed, clinking their glasses together.

As the evening wound down, Judy found herself watching Bob interact with Henry and the others who stopped by their table. There was a lightness to him she hadn't seen in years—a youthful energy that had nothing to do with physical age and everything to do with the spirit of joy he'd embraced.

She felt it too—a delicious sense of having stepped outside their comfortable routine into something unexpected and wonderful. Their performance hadn't been perfect by any technical standard, but it had been perfect in all the ways that mattered.

CHAPTER TEN

Late-afternoon light filtered through the trees as Nick and Lisa walked the perimeter of Nick's bayfront property. After the recent mystery of missing items, they'd decided to thoroughly examine the yard in daylight, hoping to find some clue about their unknown observer.

"I still can't believe the cameras didn't pick up anything," Lisa said, carefully scanning the ground where she'd seen the glowing eyes. "Those things are supposed to trigger at the slightest movement."

Nick nodded, frowning as he knelt to inspect the area near the tree line. "Maybe whoever or whatever it was stayed just out of range? Or..." He trailed off, his attention caught by something in a patch of soft earth. "Hold on. Look at this."

Lisa crouched beside him, following his gaze to what appeared to be a series of small impressions in the mud—clear prints that formed a trail leading from the woods toward the house.

"Paw prints," Nick said, his eyebrows rising. "I didn't notice these yesterday."

Lisa leaned closer. "They're tiny. Look at the shape though."

"Yeah," Nick agreed, measuring one print against his thumb. "And look at the pattern—four toes, with these little claw marks at the tips. See how they form an oval shape?"

Lisa pulled out her phone and snapped several photos of the prints from different angles. "They look fresh. Probably from last night."

They followed the trail of prints, which led toward the garage before veering off toward the side of the house where the garden lights had disappeared. The tracks then circled back toward the tree line, creating a winding path through the property.

"Whatever made these was definitely exploring," Nick said, straightening up.

Lisa scrolled through the photos she'd taken, zooming in on the clearest print. "Let me see if I can figure out what animal this might be."

While Lisa searched online, Nick continued examining the area, looking for any other signs of their nocturnal visitor. He found several more tracks near the deck stairs and what looked like fur caught on a rough piece of wood.

"Hey, come look at this," Lisa called, waving him over. "I think I've figured it out."

Nick joined her, looking over her shoulder at her phone screen. "What did you find?"

"I'm not completely certain, but these prints match what I'm seeing for fox tracks. See the distinctive chevron shape in the pad?" She showed him a diagram then swiped to compare it with the photo she'd taken. "And the spacing between the toes looks right."

"A fox?" Nick repeated, considering the possibility. "That would explain the glowing eyes you saw. But would a fox steal cushions and garden lights?"

Lisa shrugged. "Apparently some foxes are known to take objects, especially if they're preparing a den. They might be attracted to soft items or things with interesting smells."

Nick ran a hand through his hair, a bemused expression crossing his face. "So you're saying our mysterious thief might be a fox collecting furnishings for its home?"

"It's just a theory," Lisa said, "but it fits what we're seeing. The paw prints, the eyes in the dark, the missing soft items like your scarf and cushions."

Nick laughed softly. "I was expecting neighborhood kids or a disgruntled local, not wildlife."

"We need to confirm it," Lisa said, her expression brightening with determination. "Another stakeout, but this time with a better camera setup."

"And bait," Nick added, embracing the idea. "If it is a fox, we could leave something out deliberately and see if it takes it."

They spent the afternoon preparing for their second night of surveillance. Nick repositioned the trail cameras to better cover the yard and set up a small action camera on a tripod, focused on a particular spot near the tree line where they planned to place their bait.

As the afternoon light began to fade, they headed inside to prepare a quick dinner before their stakeout began.

"What should we use as bait?" Lisa asked as she chopped vegetables in the kitchen.

Nick thought for a moment. "I've got another scarf in my truck—a red one I rarely wear. If it's a fox looking for soft nesting material, that might be appealing."

After an early dinner, they positioned themselves on the deck with a clear view of the yard. The scarf had been placed casually on a low stump near the edge of the property, visible from their vantage point but not so obvious that it would appear deliberately placed.

"Now we wait," Nick said, settling into his chair with a pair of binoculars.

Lisa nodded, adjusting her own position. "And hope our little thief makes an appearance."

Time passed with nothing but the occasional rustling in the

trees and the distant calls of night birds. They maintained their watch, talking quietly and scanning the darkness for any sign of movement. The moon rose higher, casting silver light across the yard and creating deep shadows beneath the trees.

"Maybe we should call it a night," Nick suggested as boredom began to set in. "We can check the cameras in the morning."

Lisa sighed, stretching her arms above her head. "You're probably right. If our fox friend is out there, it might be avoiding us because—"

She broke off suddenly, grabbing Nick's arm. "There! By the big pine tree."

Nick raised his binoculars, focusing on the spot she'd indicated. For a moment, he saw nothing. Then a subtle movement caught his eye—a shadow detaching itself from the darkness beneath the trees.

"I see it," he whispered, hardly daring to breathe.

They watched, transfixed, as a small creature emerged cautiously from the underbrush. In the moonlight, they could make out a pointed face, alert ears, and what appeared to be reddish fur.

"It is a fox," Lisa breathed, her voice barely audible.

Nick reached for the flashlight beside him, hesitated, then decided against using it. "Let's not scare it off."

The fox paused at the edge of the clearing, nose twitching as it tested the air. After a moment of apparent deliberation, it began moving again, its path taking it directly toward the scarf they'd left out.

Lisa stifled a giggle as the animal approached the bait, its movements both cautious and curious. The fox circled the stump twice, sniffing carefully before finally approaching the scarf. With delicate precision, it picked up one end of the fabric in its mouth.

"I can't believe it," Nick whispered, grinning in the darkness. "Mystery solved."

They watched in amazement as the fox gave the scarf an experimental tug, then attempted to drag it away. The fabric caught on a protruding branch of the stump, causing the fox to pull harder, its head tilted at a comical angle as it engaged in a tug-of-war with the inanimate object.

Lisa pressed a hand to her mouth to contain her laughter. "Poor thing. It's really determined."

After several more tugs, the scarf came free, and the fox immediately began trotting away with its prize, the fabric trailing behind it like a royal train.

"Should we follow it?" Lisa asked, already rising from her chair.

Nick nodded, grabbing his flashlight. "Carefully, though. We don't want to scare it away before we see where it goes."

They descended the deck stairs quietly and kept a respectful distance as they followed the fox toward the woods. The animal moved with purpose, occasionally stopping to adjust its grip on the scarf but never dropping it.

At the edge of the property, the fox disappeared into a dense patch of underbrush. Nick and Lisa approached cautiously, using their flashlights to illuminate the area without shining them directly ahead.

"There," Nick whispered, pointing to a small opening beneath the tangled roots of an old oak tree. "I think that's its den."

Lisa directed her light toward the entrance and gasped. Scattered around the opening and partially visible within were all their missing items—the striped cushions arranged as a makeshift nest, the garden lights positioned like sentinels, Nick's gloves, the blue scarf, and even the small trowel carefully incorporated into the cozy arrangement.

"Mystery solved," Nick said, shaking his head in wonder. "And all this time we were worried about neighborhood pranksters."

They watched as the red fox added the newly acquired

scarf to its collection, arranging it with surprising care before disappearing deeper into the den.

"Should we take our stuff back?" Lisa asked, though her tone suggested she already knew the answer.

Nick looked at the carefully assembled nest then at the small paw prints leading to and from the den. After a moment, he shook his head. "Let's leave it. Looks like the little guy is preparing for winter, and honestly, I don't mind contributing to the cause."

Lisa smiled, slipping her hand into his. "That's what I was hoping you'd say."

They started back toward the house, the mystery finally solved. The evening's adventure had brought an unexpected but satisfying conclusion to their days of wondering and worrying.

"I have to admit," Nick said as they climbed the steps to the deck, "I'm relieved our neighborhood thief turned out to be a fox and not a person. Though I should probably make sure the garage door is closed all the way and locked from now on."

Lisa laughed. "And maybe we should leave out some old blankets or towels for nesting material, though I bet it would still prefer your clothes. They probably smell more interesting."

"Good idea," Nick agreed with a grin. "I'd rather donate intentionally to the fox fund than wonder what's going to disappear next."

He gazed out at the dark tree line, where somewhere their furry neighbor was settling into its newly furnished den. "Welcome to the neighborhood, little thief," he murmured. "Just leave my fishing gear alone, and we'll get along just fine."

* * *

At the marina, Chris methodically checked his supplies for the evening's tour. Around him, the hum of nearby boat engines and occasional calls between marina staff provided a familiar soundtrack to his preparations.

"Blankets, hand warmers, treats," he murmured to himself, mentally ticking off items from his list. After the last disastrous tour, he had spent days implementing Sarah's suggestions. Tonight would be different.

Inside the cabin, the transformation was remarkable. Strings of soft white lights now draped across the ceiling in gentle swags, creating a gentle, inviting glow. Additional colored lights framed the windows, transforming the previously plain space into something that actually felt festive. Chris had even found a small artificial tree that fit perfectly in the corner by the helm, decorated with miniature nautical ornaments—tiny anchors, lighthouses, shore birds, and sailboats that complemented the *Blue Heron*'s regular identity as a bird-watching tour boat.

He adjusted the volume on the newly installed speaker system, letting the cheerful notes of "Rockin' Around the Christmas Tree" fill the space at a pleasant level—loud enough to create atmosphere but not so overpowering that it would prevent conversation. The previous tour's instrumental jazz Christmas music, while tasteful, had lacked the familiar energy that could get people humming along and into the holiday spirit.

Near the entrance, Chris had arranged neat stacks of plush fleece blankets in red and green, alongside wicker baskets filled with hand warmer packets. The boat's small countertop, typically used for distributing bird guides and binoculars, now held an attractive display of seasonal treats—cranberry white chocolate bark, shortbread, and a glass jar filled with candy canes.

But perhaps most importantly, the problematic window had been properly repaired and tested. No more surprise soakings for unsuspecting passengers.

"Looking good, *Blue Heron*," Chris said, patting the wheel affectionately. "Let's redeem ourselves tonight."

As the clock ticked closer to departure time, Chris changed into a nicer version of his captain's attire, adding a small Santa hat pin to his jacket. The extra touch of festivity seemed appropriate given the occasion, and he wanted customers to feel they were getting more than just a standard boat tour with a few Christmas lights thrown in.

Wind whistled through the dock as the first guests arrived fifteen minutes early, a middle-aged couple bundled in matching navy parkas.

"Welcome aboard the *Blue Heron*!" Chris greeted them with genuine enthusiasm, gesturing toward the small counter. "Please help yourself to some seasonal snacks before we depart."

The couple nodded appreciatively, their expressions registering pleasant surprise as they stepped into the twinkling cabin.

"This is lovely," the woman remarked, selecting a piece of cranberry bark and glancing around at the holiday decorations. "So cozy!"

"Please take a hand warmer packet," Chris offered, gesturing to the baskets. "And there are blankets available if you'd like one once we get moving. It can still get chilly out on the water this time of year."

The woman's husband nodded with approval. "Smart thinking. We brought extra layers, but a blanket sounds perfect."

More passengers arrived in quick succession—a family with two elementary-aged children, an older couple who moved slowly but beamed at the decorations, and several other pairs and small groups until all seats for the evening's tour were filled. The cabin hummed with conversation and anticipation, a stark contrast to the strained silence of the previous journey.

"Welcome aboard, everyone," Chris announced, taking his

position at the steering console. "I'm Chris, your captain for tonight's tour of the back bay's decorated waterfront properties. We'll stop midway at the Hot Chocolate Shack for complimentary refreshments and have you back by eight-thirty."

As the *Blue Heron* pulled away from the dock, "Deck the Halls" began playing through the speakers. The lights inside the cabin seemed to shine more vibrantly as darkness fell around them, and several passengers immediately reached for blankets, draping them across laps with expressions of contentment rather than the desperate attempt to ward off cold that Chris had witnessed days prior.

"Our first stop is coming up on the right," Chris announced, slowing the boat as they approached a handsome gray-shingled house set back from a spacious lawn that sloped down to the water. "The Carmichael home features a nautical Christmas theme this year."

The waterfront property was outlined in blue and white illumination that reflected off the dark water, creating a magical doubling effect. On the lawn, a large glowing anchor stood alongside a sailboat wrapped entirely in white bulbs, while a sea of smaller blue pinpoints mimicked gentle waves beneath the vessel.

"Oh, look at that!" one woman exclaimed, pointing to where a light-wrapped dinghy floated at the dock, filled with wrapped packages and a smiling illuminated snowman as its passenger.

Passengers moved to the windows, cameras and phones at the ready, capturing the scene with evident delight. Some had left their blankets behind in the comfort of the cabin, while others kept them draped around their shoulders as they snapped photos.

"The Carmichaels have lived here for twenty years," Chris narrated, feeling a surge of confidence at the positive response. "Mr. Carmichael was a navy captain before retirement, which explains his commitment to the nautical theme. They add something new to the display each year."

As they continued along the shoreline, Chris guided the boat past a series of decorated homes, each with its own charm and style. His narrative flowed smoothly now, mixing historical tidbits about the properties with personal anecdotes about the homeowners who had granted permission to be included on the tour.

"Coming up next is something quite unexpected for Back Bay," Chris announced as they approached a brightly lit property on a curved section of shoreline. "The Mitchell family refuses to let a Jersey Shore winter interfere with their love of a tropical Christmas."

Even from the water, the display was captivating. The traditional colonial home was surrounded by palm trees wrapped in lights, their fronds outlined in bright green. Pink flamingo lawn ornaments sporting Santa hats and beards stood in illuminated formation across the yard, while inflatable palm trees with Christmas lights flanked the dock.

"Mrs. Mitchell is originally from Key West," Chris explained, "and this is her way of bringing a bit of Florida paradise to our New Jersey winters."

The children on board pressed their faces against the windows, giggling at the flamingos. Their parents seemed equally entertained, pointing out various details to each other as Chris slowly navigated past the property.

"They've been doing the tropical theme for eight years," Chris continued. "The spectacle has become so popular that it's now one of the highlights of the local driving tour. People come from miles around just to see their flamingo Santa parade."

The boat moved deeper into the bay, passing more traditionally decorated homes with varying levels of elaboration. Some featured simple white lights outlining rooflines and windows, while others displayed colorful lights and illuminated deer, snowmen, and sleighs across expansive waterfront lawns.

"Now we're approaching what many consider the crown jewel of the back bay's Christmas displays," Chris announced, slowing the boat to a near stop. "The Andersons' synchronized light show."

Chris tapped a button on his phone, and the cabin speakers began playing "Carol of the Bells," perfectly timed to match the display ahead. As they watched, the massive waterfront property suddenly went dark. A few passengers murmured in anticipation, having heard about this display. Then, a single white light appeared at the center of the house, growing and branching outward in perfect synchronization with the energetic melody now filling the cabin.

"They broadcast the music on a special AM frequency for cars viewing from the street," Chris explained quietly, not wanting to distract from the spectacle unfolding before them. "The Andersons designed this display to be enjoyed from both land and water. We're actually getting the better view from the bay."

The display built in perfect synchronization with the music —thousands of bulbs flashing, chasing, and dancing across the property. The entire facade of the three-story home transformed into an illuminated canvas, with patterns flowing like water one moment and bursting like fireworks the next. When the music reached its crescendo, every light on the property— house, trees, lawn, and dock—flashed in perfect unison, reflecting off the bay waters to create an immersive dome of brilliance surrounding the viewers.

"Wow," breathed one of the children, the simple word seeming to capture the sentiment of everyone aboard.

Chris allowed the boat to linger until the six-minute show concluded, knowing from experience that a new cycle wouldn't begin for another fifteen minutes. As they pulled away, the cabin buzzed with excited conversation.

"That was incredible!"

"Did you see how the lights made shapes on the lawn?"

"I've never seen anything like it before!"

Chris smiled to himself as he guided the *Blue Heron* toward their next destination, the previous week's disaster feeling increasingly distant. Ahead, he could make out the figure of Ed Foster—a retired firefighter with a remarkable resemblance to Santa Claus—standing on his waterfront deck in full costume, ready to wave at the tour boat as it passed.

"Ladies and gentlemen," Chris announced, "I believe that's Santa himself up ahead, taking a break from toy-making to enjoy the waterfront view."

On cue, Santa raised both arms in an enthusiastic wave as the *Blue Heron* approached. The children squealed with delight, and the adults waved back with enthusiasm, caught up in the simple joy of the moment.

"Now we'll head to our scheduled refreshment stop," Chris announced, turning the boat toward the marina. "It's about five minutes away."

The boat cruised smoothly through the bay, passing a few more decorated waterfront homes as they made their way back toward the marina. Soon, the pier came into view with the small cabin at its edge, windows glimmering invitingly.

"Here we are at the Hot Chocolate Shack," Chris announced, carefully maneuvering alongside the pier. "Fifteen minutes to heat up before we continue."

As Chris secured the boat to the marina pier, passengers began gathering their things, ready for the promised refreshment break.

The tiny wooden structure that served as the Hot Chocolate Shack was even more charming up close. It was essentially a shed-like cabin at the end of the pier, with a serving window now thrown open to welcome visitors. Evergreen garlands framed the window, intertwined with lights that matched the golden glow spilling from inside. A wreath fashioned from driftwood and seashells hung beside the window, adding a coastal holiday flair to the humble structure.

"Welcome to the Hot Chocolate Shack!" a woman with long blond hair called out cheerfully from the window as the tour group approached. "I'm Nicki. Step right up, and I'll have your drinks ready in a jiffy."

"Nicki runs this place year-round," Chris explained to the group. "She agreed to partner with me for these tours, and she makes the best hot chocolate you'll ever taste."

Nicki efficiently distributed steaming paper cups of hot chocolate, each topped with a generous dollop of homemade marshmallow that slowly melted into the rich liquid beneath.

"Time to continue our tour, folks!" Chris announced after everyone had received their drinks. "We've got more beautiful displays ahead."

The passengers, carefully balancing their hot chocolates, made their way back to the boat.

Back aboard the *Blue Heron*, the pleasant atmosphere continued as Chris guided the boat through the remainder of the tour. Over the next half hour, they cruised past several more decorated waterfront homes – from a historic Victorian with elegant white lights to a Cape Cod-style home featuring entirely handcrafted decorations.

For the grand finale, Chris steered them toward a spectacular display celebrating Cape May's heritage, with illuminated figures of the town's iconic trolley, lighthouse, Victorian buildings, and even a large butterfly display representing the famous local monarch migration. The passengers oohed and aahed at this final show of lights, many taking photos to remember the experience.

As they left the final display behind and the *Blue Heron* made its way back toward the marina, Chris took a moment to appreciate how different this experience had been from his first attempt. The simple changes Sarah had suggested had transformed a disaster into what appeared to be a genuine success.

"Ladies and gentlemen, we're approaching the marina to conclude our Christmas Lights Tour," Chris announced. "I want to thank you for joining me tonight and hope you've enjoyed seeing the back bay's holiday decorations from this unique perspective."

To his surprise and delight, the passengers broke into spontaneous applause.

"This was wonderful," called out the mother of the two children. "The kids haven't stopped talking about the lights and that amazing hot chocolate."

"Such a pleasant evening," added the older gentleman, his wife nodding in agreement beside him. "Much more enjoyable than fighting traffic to see the displays by car."

As the boat docked and passengers began gathering their belongings, Chris stood by the exit to bid each person farewell. To his further gratification, a middle-aged couple lingered after most had departed.

"We have family visiting from Chicago next week," the woman explained. "Is there any chance you have space available for another tour? They would absolutely love this experience."

"Absolutely," Chris replied, trying to contain his excitement at the prospect of repeat business. "I'll be running these tours through New Year's—every evening except Christmas Eve and Christmas Day."

After taking down their information and confirming the booking, Chris watched the last of his passengers make their way back to the parking lot, their voices carrying in the night air as they continued to discuss their favorite displays. When the final car pulled away, he allowed himself a moment of pure, unrestrained satisfaction.

He pulled out his phone and dialed Sarah's number. When she answered, he didn't even wait for her greeting.

"It worked," he said, unable to keep the elation from his voice. "Everything you suggested—it all worked perfectly."

CHAPTER ELEVEN

Margaret stood on the front porch of their beach house with Harper and Abby, adjusting the final strand of white lights that Dave had woven through the evergreen garland draped along the railing.

"Does that look straight to you?" Margaret asked, stepping back to examine their work.

"Perfect, Mom," Harper said, while Abby nodded in agreement.

The transformation was complete—their little cottage had been dressed for Christmas with understated elegance.

"The porch looks beautiful from out here!" Dave called from the yard, where he was positioning luminaries along the walkway.

Margaret stepped back and looked up at her handiwork. The soft lights twinkled against the deep green of the fresh pine garland, while matching swags adorned each window. Red velvet bows scattered throughout added just the right touch of color. "I'm glad!" she called back. "It looks wonderful from here too."

With the outdoor decorations complete, Margaret headed inside with Harper and Abby to make final preparations.

The house had been transformed into a Christmas wonderland. The gorgeous blue spruce they'd selected from Tom Wilson's farm filled the corner of the living room by the front window, its eight-foot height reaching nearly to the ceiling. Margaret had spent hours decorating it with a mix of their treasured family ornaments and new ones they'd discovered in Cape May's antique shops—vintage glass balls in deep jewel tones, delicate silver snowflakes, and vintage multicolor light strings.

The fresh pine scent that permeated every corner of the house created an instant Christmas atmosphere that took Margaret back to childhood memories of her grandmother's house during the holidays. Christmas music played softly in the background.

"The seafood catering is here!" Dave announced, coming through the front door with his arms full of warming trays, followed by a caterer carrying chafing dishes. "There's more in the van," Dave added.

Margaret clapped her hands together in excitement. She'd planned a seafood feast—snow crab legs, jumbo shrimp, littleneck clams, and fresh fish fillets. The buffet tables in the dining room were already set with festive red and gold linens, evergreen centerpieces dotted with white candles, and stacks of plates waiting for the evening's bounty.

"Perfect timing," she said, directing the delivery to the kitchen. "Let's get everything prepped and ready to go."

The kitchen counters were already crowded with appetizers and desserts she'd been preparing. Spinach-and-artichoke dip bubbled in the slow cooker, while trays of bacon-wrapped scallops waited in the refrigerator. Her famous sugar cookies were arranged on tiered stands, and a chocolate trifle sat chilling alongside several bottles of champagne. A large pot of spiced wine punch simmered on the stove, filling the kitchen with the warm scents of cinnamon and cloves.

"I can't believe we're actually doing this," Margaret said,

feeling a flutter of nervous excitement as she checked her watch. People would start arriving soon.

Dave wrapped his arms around her from behind, resting his chin on her shoulder. "It's going to be wonderful. The house looks incredible, the food smells amazing, and the company will be perfect."

Margaret leaned back against him, taking a moment to appreciate what they'd accomplished. In just a few months, they'd transformed this weathered cottage into an inviting, welcoming home. And tonight, they would fill it with friends, family, and neighbors, creating new memories.

As the sun began to set and the evening grew colder, Margaret made final adjustments to the food presentation while Dave built a fire in the living room fireplace. The flames danced in the hearth, adding another layer of warmth and ambiance to the already cozy space.

The first knock on the door came at exactly six o'clock. Margaret smoothed her red sweater and checked her reflection in the hallway mirror before opening the door to find Liz and Greg standing on the porch with their sons Steven and Michael, each adult carrying covered dishes.

"Merry Christmas Eve!" Liz exclaimed, pulling Margaret into a hug. "The house looks absolutely magical from the street."

"Come in, come in," Margaret said, ushering them inside. "Let me take those dishes."

Liz had brought her famous crab dip and homemade dinner rolls, while Greg carried a bottle of wine and what appeared to be a dessert container. "My specialty bread pudding," Greg said as he handed over the warm dish.

Dave appeared to greet them, and soon they were settled in the living room with glasses of champagne, wine, and mugs of spiced wine punch, admiring the Christmas tree and catching up on each other's holiday plans. The conversation flowed easily, and Margaret felt herself beginning to relax into the rhythm of hosting. Harper and Abby had retreated to the back porch with a stack of board games, joined by Steven and Michael.

The next arrivals were Donna and Dale, bearing gifts of delicious appetizers. Donna's chocolate-bourbon bread pudding and Dale's lobster bisque were exactly the special touches their feast needed.

"This place is stunning," Donna said, looking around the transformed living space. "I can't believe it's the same house we saw when you first bought it."

"It's been a labor of love," Dave said proudly, refilling glasses as more guests began to arrive.

Judy and Bob appeared next, accompanied by a distinguished gentleman whom Margaret had never met before.

"Margaret, Dave, I'd like you to meet our friend Henry," Judy said. "Henry, this is our daughter Margaret and her husband, Dave."

Henry's handshake was firm, and his smile was genuine. "What a wonderful thing you're doing," he said, "opening your home to friends and family for the holidays."

Margaret found herself immediately charmed by Henry.

Nick and Lisa arrived shortly after, both animated and eager to share news about their latest discovery.

"You'll never guess what we figured out at the bay house," Lisa said, barely pausing to hand over their coats. "We've had a thief stealing things from the property, and it turns out it's a fox! We've been tracking it for days."

"It's been taking small items and stashing them somewhere," Nick added with a grin. "We finally caught it in the act yesterday."

The conversation about the fox drew everyone into an animated discussion about local wildlife and unusual animal encounters they'd had over the years.

Sarah and Chris were the next to arrive, bringing with them the easy camaraderie that Margaret always enjoyed.

Sarah carried a beautiful poinsettia centerpiece, while Chris brought a large tray of homemade stuffed mushrooms.

"The snow is starting to fall," Sarah mentioned casually as she removed her coat. "Just a light dusting, but it's so pretty in the streetlights."

Margaret glanced toward the windows but could see nothing beyond the Christmas lights reflected in the glass. She made a mental note to step outside later to enjoy the snow but was quickly distracted by the need to coordinate the food service as more neighbors and friends continued to arrive.

The house filled with chatter and laughter as people moved between rooms, admiring the decorations, sampling appetizers, and sharing holiday stories. Margaret had worried about having enough space, but the cozy layout of the main level accommodated the growing crowd perfectly, with people naturally gravitating toward different areas—some gathered around the fireplace, others clustered in the kitchen, sampling food, and several couples wandering out to the screened porch, where the kids had congregated with their board games.

Just as Margaret was beginning to think about serving the main course, Tom and Nanette Wilson appeared at the front door, both looking slightly overwhelmed by the bustle of the party but pleased to be included, brushing light snow from their coats.

"We can't stay long," Tom said apologetically as Margaret welcomed them inside, helping them with their coats. "We're expected at our son's house for dinner with the grandkids, but we wanted to stop by and see how that beautiful blue spruce looks in your living room. That snow's really starting to come down out there."

Nanette beamed as she took in the decorated tree. "Oh my goodness, Tom, look how perfectly it fits in that corner. It's like it was meant to be there."

Margaret guided them through the crowd, introducing them to the other guests and making sure they could sample a few appetizers. She was touched that they'd made the effort to come, knowing they had family dinner plans.

"This tree came from the Wilson farm," Margaret announced to the gathered crowd, her arm around Nanette's shoulders. "Tom and his family have been growing Christmas trees in Cape May for over fifty years."

The revelation sparked a conversation about local businesses and family traditions, with several guests sharing memories of their own childhood experiences choosing Christmas trees at various farms around the area. Tom found himself surrounded by interested listeners as he described the process of growing and maintaining the evergreens, clearly enjoying the genuine curiosity about his life's work.

"We should get going," Nanette said eventually, squeezing Margaret's hand. "This has been wonderful, but Tom's right—we do have family expecting us."

Margaret walked them to the door, grateful they'd been able to share even a brief part of the evening. "Thank you for coming, and thank you for the most beautiful Christmas tree we've ever had." As she opened the door, she noticed the snow was falling more steadily now, though it still looked manageable—maybe an inch or so coating the walkway and cars.

As Tom and Nanette disappeared into the night, Margaret removed the covers from the seafood feast. The warming trays kept everything at perfect temperature in the dining room, where she had arranged everything buffet-style. The snow crab legs were piled high on platters with small bowls of drawn butter, while the shrimp formed an elegant display around a tangy cocktail sauce. The clams had been steamed to perfection, and Dale's lobster bisque simmered in a large pot with a ladle for easy serving.

The feast was complemented by carefully chosen side dishes—pasta salad with fresh herbs, mixed greens with pomegranate seeds and candied pecans, and warm dinner rolls that Liz had brought. Everything was designed to be eaten casually, allowing people to fill their plates and continue socializing without the formality of a sit-down dinner.

"This is incredible," Henry said, his plate loaded with crab legs and shrimp. "I haven't had seafood this fresh in years."

Margaret smiled. "Thank you, Henry."

She moved through the crowd, making sure glasses stayed full and empty plates were replaced, but mostly just enjoying the sight of her friends and neighbors savoring both the food and each other's company.

Outside, the snow that Sarah had mentioned earlier was beginning to fall more steadily, though no one seemed to notice as they were too absorbed in the warmth and festivities inside. The conversations flowed from topic to topic—holiday traditions, local history, travel stories, and shared memories of Cape May in different seasons.

Nearly two hours later, Margaret stepped outside briefly to retrieve more firewood from the stack Dave had built along the side of the house, wanting to keep the fireplace burning brightly throughout the evening. She expected to see the inch or so of snow she'd noticed when Tom and Nanette left, but what greeted her instead made her gasp in surprise.

Six inches of snow had already accumulated on the ground, coating the cars, the walkway, and the carefully placed luminaries. The flakes were falling thick and fast, creating an almost magical winter wonderland but also raising immediate concerns about her guests' ability to get home safely.

The forecast had only called for a light dusting—an inch at most. This was clearly something much more significant.

She hurried back inside, setting the firewood by the hearth before finding Dave in the kitchen, where he was putting out more silverware and napkins.

"Dave," she said quietly, pulling him aside. "We need to talk. Come look outside."

Dave followed her to the sliding glass doors, his eyes widening as he took in the transformed landscape. "That's a lot more than a dusting," he said, pulling out his phone to check the weather forecast and road conditions.

Margaret watched his expression grow more serious as he scrolled through updates. "What are you seeing?"

"The coastal storm intensified unexpectedly," he said, showing her the weather radar on his phone. "Roads are unplowed and getting treacherous. They're saying another six inches expected before morning."

They looked at each other, the same realization dawning simultaneously. Most of their guests wouldn't be able to get home safely, especially those who lived farther inland or had to cross bridges.

"What do we do?" Margaret asked, though part of her already knew the answer.

Dave glanced around at their house full of friends then back at the steadily falling snow outside. "I think we make an announcement and hope everyone has a sense of humor about unexpected sleepovers."

Margaret felt a flutter of panic mixed with excitement. They had three bedrooms in the beach house, plus the screened porch and living room areas. With some creative arrangements, they could accommodate everyone, but it would require cooperation and good humor from their guests.

"Should we tell them?" she asked.

Dave nodded. "Better to address it now than wait until people try to leave and realize they can't."

He moved to the center of the living room, gently tapping his wine glass with a spoon to get everyone's attention. The conversations gradually died down as people turned toward him expectantly.

"I hate to interrupt the party," Dave began with a smile, "but we've got a situation outside that I think everyone should know about. Take a look."

He gestured toward the windows, and several people

moved closer to peer out into the night. Gasps and exclamations arose as they took in the heavy snowfall.

"The forecast completely missed this one," Dave continued. "We've got about six inches already, and it's coming down fast. The roads are unplowed and dangerous. So..." He paused, meeting Margaret's eyes with a grin. "Looks like we're all having a Christmas Eve sleepover!"

There was a moment of stunned silence, followed by nervous laughter as most of the guests moved toward the front door to see for themselves. They stepped out onto the front porch without bothering with jackets, exclamations of surprise and disbelief arising as they took in the heavy accumulation and still-falling snow before quickly retreating back inside from the cold.

"Actually," Henry said with a smile, "I think I'll just walk home. I only live a few blocks away, and I've walked in worse weather than this."

"Are you sure?" Bob asked, concerned.

"Absolutely," Henry replied, already reaching for his coat. "Thank you for a wonderful evening."

After Henry bundled up and headed out into the snow, Harper and Abby's excited voices broke through the chatter. "A sleepover!" Abby exclaimed. "This is like the best Christmas Eve ever!"

"Can we go out and play in it?" Harper asked eagerly. Steven and Michael were already reaching for their coats, clearly planning to head outside as well.

"Just for a little while," Margaret said, "since you don't have proper snow gear."

"We don't care!" Harper and Abby chorused, while Steven and Michael nodded eagerly, and soon all four were bundling up in whatever coats and shoes they had, rushing outside to experience the magical snowfall. Harper and Abby's shrieks of delight could be heard from inside as they caught snowflakes and spun around in the falling snow, while Steven and Michael good-naturedly joined in, tossing snowballs and grinning despite trying to act cool. Soon they all retreated back to the warmth of the house, cheeks red and eyes sparkling.

Their enthusiasm was contagious, and soon genuine excitement spread through the group as the magical nature of the situation began to sink in.

Margaret found herself organizing sleeping arrangements with the efficiency of a cruise director, while Dave disappeared into closets to retrieve air mattresses and spare bedding.

"Judy and Bob, you take the master bedroom," Margaret announced. "Sarah and Chris, you get the second bedroom. Donna and Dale, the small third bedroom is yours. Dave and I can set up in the dining room with Harper and Abby in sleeping bags. Steven and Michael, you can have the winterized back porch, and Nick, Lisa, Liz and Greg, you can share the living room with the pull-out sofa and air mattresses."

Dave emerged with an armload of spare pajamas, toothbrushes still in packages, and travel-sized toiletries. "The benefits of having daughters," he explained with a grin. "I've learned to keep emergency supplies for unexpected sleepovers."

The party seamlessly transitioned into a cozy overnight gathering as people changed into borrowed pajamas and settled into their temporary accommodations. Soon everyone had gathered back downstairs in their sleepwear - those staying in the upstairs bedrooms joining the group in the living room. Margaret couldn't help but laugh at the sight of Greg wearing a pair of Dave's flannel pajamas that were slightly too big for him, while Steven and Michael had ended up in some of Dave's old college T-shirts that served as makeshift pajamas.

"This is surreal," Donna said, settling onto one of the air mattresses in the living room. "I feel like we're all at summer camp."

Someone had turned up the Christmas music, and the soft melodies filled the house as snow continued to pile up against the windows. The fireplace cast a warm glow over the group of friends now gathered in mismatched pajamas, creating an intimate atmosphere that felt both absurd and absolutely perfect.

"You know what we need?" Judy said, settling into one of the comfortable chairs near the fireplace. "Christmas stories. Everyone should share a favorite Christmas memory."

Everyone agreed this was a perfect idea, and soon the group was arranged in a comfortable circle around the fireplace, some on chairs, others on the floor with pillows and blankets. Margaret dimmed the overhead lights, leaving only the tree lights and the fireplace to illuminate their faces.

Bob, as one of the eldest members of the group, was naturally elected to go first. His voice took on a storytelling cadence as he began to share memories of Christmas during his childhood in the 1950s, when families would gather around the television to watch holiday specials and children treasured toys like cap guns, model trains, and dolls that came in beautifully illustrated boxes.

"I remember one Christmas when I was eight," he said, his eyes reflecting the firelight. "We lived in a small town in Pennsylvania, and there was a blizzard much like this one. My father couldn't get home from work, and my mother was worried sick. But the neighbors all came together, sharing food and stories, making sure no one was alone. It ended up being one of the most magical Christmases of my childhood."

His story prompted others to share their own memories—childhood traditions, family gatherings, memorable gifts, and holiday disasters that had become beloved family legends. Margaret found herself laughing until her sides hurt at Greg's story of the year his family's Christmas tree fell over in the middle of Christmas morning, crushing half the presents and creating chaos that became the subject of family jokes for decades.

The flickering flames illuminated their faces as snow piled up against the windows, creating a sense of being cocooned in warmth and friendship while the winter storm raged outside.

Margaret looked around at her friends and family—all gathered in borrowed pajamas, sharing intimate stories and creating new memories together.

"This is perfect," she murmured to Dave during a lull in the storytelling.

"Better than perfect," he agreed, pulling her closer on the couch they were sharing. "This is the kind of Christmas Eve you remember for the rest of your life."

As the evening wore on and the stories gradually gave way to comfortable silence, people began to drift toward their sleeping arrangements. Margaret moved through the house, making sure everyone had enough blankets and pillows, checking that the fire was safely banked, and turning off lights throughout the house.

The last thing she did before settling in for the night was step out onto the front porch to check the snow one more time. The world had been transformed into a winter wonderland, with drifts reaching nearly to the porch railings and snow still falling steadily in the glow of the Christmas lights.

She found Dave in the dining room, having finished setting up their makeshift bed and now looking out the window at the snow-covered landscape.

"Can you believe this?" she said quietly.

"I'm starting to think this house has its own kind of magic," Dave replied, sitting down on their air mattress and patting the space beside him. "We end up with a house full of friends snowed in on Christmas Eve. It's like something out of a movie. And this is the first white Christmas I can remember since I was a kid."

Margaret curled up against him, listening to the soft sounds of their friends settling in throughout the house—quiet conversations from the other bedrooms, someone moving around in the kitchen, getting a glass of water, the gentle creak of the old house adjusting to its unexpected occupancy.

"Do you think this might be our most memorable Christmas ever?" she asked softly.

Dave kissed the top of her head, pulling the blankets up around them both. "I think this is exactly what Christmas Eve should be. This house filled with people who care about each other, everyone safe and warm while the snow falls outside."

As Margaret drifted off to sleep, she thought about how the evening had unfolded—their carefully planned party transforming into something completely unexpected but infinitely more magical.

CHAPTER TWELVE

Sunlight glistened across the snowy landscape as Christmas morning dawned at the beach house. Margaret woke early on the air mattress in the dining room, drawn to the brilliant light filtering through the curtains. She padded to the window and smiled at the breathtaking scene, feeling the chill of cold air seeping through the glass. The Cape May snow had continued through the night, and now in the morning sun, everything sparkled like diamonds. The Victorian houses of their neighborhood were transformed into frosted gingerbread creations, their ornate details highlighted by pristine white.

She wrapped her robe tighter and slipped quietly from the dining room, careful not to wake Dave, Harper, and Abby, or any of the guests sleeping throughout the first floor. The house was still quiet, with people presumably still sleeping both upstairs and in the living room. When she entered the kitchen, she was surprised to find Liz already dressed and peering out the window.

"Merry Christmas," she said, turning to Margaret with a smile. "Roads are clear. County must have had the plows out all night. Greg's checking the weather app now, but we should be able to get on the road pretty soon."

"So soon?" Margaret couldn't hide her surprise. "I was planning to make everyone breakfast."

Liz shook her head. "We really should get back. Greg's parents are expecting us by noon, and with this snow, even with clear roads, we should leave a buffer."

Within the hour, the house was buzzing with activity as everybody gathered their belongings and prepared to depart. Margaret found herself standing in the entryway, accepting quick hugs and rushed thank-yous as people filed out to their cars.

"The cookies were amazing," Donna said, embracing Margaret quickly. "Next year, I want the recipe!"

"Thank you for everything," Dale added, following her out the door. "It was magical."

Margaret barely had time to wave goodbye to them before turning back to the entryway, where Chris and Sarah were preparing to leave.

"Sorry to dash off so early," Chris said, adjusting his rumpled clothes from yesterday. "The storm threw off our whole schedule."

"We had such a wonderful time," Sarah added, squeezing Margaret's hands affectionately. "This was the perfect impromptu Christmas Eve, even if we weren't prepared to stay over."

As Chris and Sarah headed out to their car, Margaret turned to find her parents gathering their things by the door, the last of the overnight guests preparing to leave.

"We hate to rush off, sweetie," Judy said as she hugged her daughter goodbye. "But we promised your Aunt Anne we'd make it to her Christmas brunch."

"The roads are clear now, so we should get there in time," Bob added, giving Margaret a quick kiss on the cheek.

Harper and Abby, still in their Christmas pajamas, appeared from the kitchen, where they'd been helping themselves to leftover Christmas cookies for breakfast. Judy bent down to hug each of them.

"Bye, girls! We'll see you soon," Bob said, ruffling Harper's hair. "Have fun with your presents."

Margaret nodded, understanding but a little disappointed. She watched as they hurried to their car, the girls waving enthusiastically beside her from the porch. As the car pulled away from the curb, leaving only tracks in the fresh snow, Margaret ushered the girls back inside, closed the front door, and leaned against it, suddenly aware of the silence that filled the house.

Dave emerged from the bathroom, still in his pajamas and robe, his hair damp from a quick shower. "Did everyone leave already?"

"They did," Margaret said. "Roads are clear, and everyone had places to be."

"So it's just us," Dave said, opening his arms. Margaret walked into his embrace, feeling the comfort of him.

"Just us," she agreed. "The original beach house crew."

Harper and Abby came into the living room, still in their Christmas pajamas. They seemed more relieved than disappointed about the quick departure of their guests.

"Can we open presents now?" Harper asked, eyeing the stack of gifts under the tree.

"Breakfast first," Margaret insisted. "I made cinnamon rolls yesterday, and they just need to go in the oven."

The kitchen felt especially cozy after the bustle of company. Dave made hot chocolate while Margaret warmed the cinnamon rolls. The girls set the table, arguing good-naturedly about which Christmas mugs each person should get.

The sweet aroma of cinnamon and sugar filled the kitchen as Margaret pulled the golden-brown rolls from the oven and drizzled them with icing. Soon they were all seated around the table, enjoying the warm, gooey treats.

"I think this is even better than our regular Christmas

morning," Abby said, licking icing from her fingers. "It's like having two Christmases."

"And we get the whole day to ourselves," Harper added. "No rushing to Grandma's or anything."

After breakfast, they gathered around the Christmas tree. Without the pressure of guests or timetables, the gift opening became an unhurried celebration. Each present was examined and appreciated fully before moving to the next. Harper and Abby's excitement filled the room as they discovered their gifts, spreading them out on the floor around them.

"A new sketchbook!" Harper held up the leather-bound book Margaret had found at an art store in Philadelphia. "And these pencils are the exact ones I wanted!"

Abby was equally delighted with her gifts, especially the collection of young adult novels Margaret had purchased at the Book Nook, based on Sarah's recommendations. "These will last me at least a week," she said, already flipping through the first one.

Dave built a fire in the fireplace while the girls examined their gifts more closely. Margaret watched her family from her spot on the couch, a contentment settling over her that she hadn't expected to feel in this new setting.

"What are you thinking about?" Dave asked, joining her after the fire was crackling satisfactorily.

"Just thinking about how perfectly everything turned out," Margaret admitted. "Even if it was different than we planned."

"Sometimes different is exactly what we need," Dave said, putting his arm around her shoulders.

The afternoon stretched before them with no obligations. As the day progressed, Margaret prepared a simple Christmas early dinner of honey-glazed ham, scalloped potatoes, and green beans, much less elaborate than the previous night's feast. They ate in the living room, plates balanced on their laps, while watching "A Christmas Story" on the television.

"This is my favorite," Harper explained to Abby, who had somehow never seen the classic film before.

Dave quoted one of the movie's famous lines along with the characters, making the girls giggle.

After lunch, they continued their movie marathon, moving from one Christmas classic to another. Harper and Abby snuggled under blankets with fresh mugs of hot cocoa and the cookies left over from the party. Margaret found herself dozing off during "Miracle on 34th Street," lulled by the fullness of food and the warmth of the fire.

As night began to creep in outside the windows, Dave stretched and stood up. "What do you say we go for a walk? See some of the neighborhood Christmas lights?"

"In the snow?" Abby asked, her expression both dubious and intrigued.

"Especially in the snow," Dave insisted. "Christmas lights look magical reflecting off snow."

They bundled up in layers, pulling on whatever shoes they had and coats, wrapping scarves around necks, and tugging hats over ears. Margaret found extra pairs of gloves in the hall closet, and soon they were ready to venture out into the winter landscape.

The snow-covered Victorian houses of Cape May looked like they'd been plucked straight from a Christmas card. Streetlamps illuminated the snow-laden trees and decorated porches. Colored lights reflected off the pristine snow, creating a kaleidoscope effect that was indeed magical, just as Dave had promised.

"Look at that one." Harper pointed to a particularly grand house with a full display of lights outlining every architectural feature. "It's like a gingerbread house."

They walked slowly, admiring each decorated home, their shoes crunching in the snow. The streets were quiet, most families still indoors celebrating their own Christmas traditions. But as they turned down an unfamiliar street, they heard laughter in the distance.

"What's that?" Abby asked, tilting her head to listen.

"Let's find out," Dave suggested, leading them toward the sound.

Behind one of the grand houses, they discovered the source of the merriment: a perfect sledding hill. Neighborhood families had gathered with sleds, toboggans, and snowboards. Children raced down the slope while adults chatted by a portable fire pit set up at the bottom of the hill.

"Oh, look!" Abby's eyes widened at the scene before them.

As they stood watching, a woman detached herself from the group by the fire and approached them. "Well, if it isn't the new beach house family," she said cheerfully. "Margaret and Dave, right?"

Margaret recognized her as one of the neighbors they'd met briefly during the fall. "Yes, hello! Merry Christmas."

"Merry Christmas! I'm Mary. We met briefly at the farmers market back in October, I think. You should join us! This is a neighborhood tradition whenever we get enough snow, which isn't often."

Before Margaret could formulate a response, a man joined them, carrying several plastic sleds. "We've got some spares if you want to try," he offered. "The hill's perfect today."

Harper and Abby looked up at Dave and Margaret with pleading eyes.

"Go ahead." Dave laughed, taking two of the offered sleds and handing them to the girls. "Just be careful!"

The girls didn't need to be told twice. They rushed to join the other children on the hill, quickly integrating into the group as only kids can do. Margaret and Dave made their way to the fire pit, where they were greeted warmly and offered cups of hot chocolate with marshmallows.

"We've been doing this for years," Mary explained. "Any

decent snowfall, and someone texts the neighborhood group. Within an hour, half the street is out here."

"It's wonderful," Margaret said, watching as Harper and Abby took their first runs down the hill, their excited shrieks joining the chorus of laughter.

Dave couldn't resist for long. After finishing his drink, he grabbed one of the remaining sleds. "I have to try this," he told Margaret with a boyish grin before joining the line at the top of the hill.

Margaret watched, laughing, as her husband careened down the slope with childlike abandon, narrowly avoiding a collision with a snowman at the bottom. He walked over to her, snow clinging to his coat, his face flushed with exertion and joy.

"Your turn," he insisted, holding out the sled to Margaret.

"Oh, I don't think so," she began, but the encouraging calls from the neighbors and the expectant looks from her daughters broke down her resistance.

"Fine," she conceded, taking the sled. "But if I break something, you're all to blame."

The climb to the top of the hill left her breathless, but the view from there was worth it. The entire neighborhood spread out before her, lights twinkling through the snowy dusk. She positioned the sled, took a deep breath, and pushed off.

The rush was immediate and exhilarating. The wind stung her cheeks as she picked up speed, the world blurring around her. She heard herself shrieking with joy, unable to contain the pure childish delight of the moment. When she finally slid to a stop at the bottom, she was laughing so hard she could barely stand.

"Again!" she declared, already heading back up the hill.

They spent hours sledding, conversing with neighbors, and sharing stories around the fire pit. The beach house Christmas they had been so excited about had transformed into something even more magical and unexpected than they'd imagined. As night fell, the sledding crowd began to thin.

"We should head back," Margaret said reluctantly, noticing how Abby was trying to hide her yawns. "It's getting late."

Their walk home through the snowy streets was quiet, their cheeks rosy from cold and laughter. The girls chattered excitedly about their unexpected sledding adventure, comparing their fastest runs and the new friends they'd made.

"Mary said we could come back tomorrow if the snow doesn't melt," Harper said. "Can we, Mom?"

"We'll see," Margaret promised, though she was already planning to return. The spontaneous neighborhood gathering had been the perfect capstone to their Christmas day.

The beach house came into view, warm light spilling from the windows they'd left illuminated. Margaret felt a surge of affection for the place that had so quickly become their holiday home.

She reached for Dave's hand as they approached the front walk. "Thank you," she said quietly.

"For what?"

"For everything. Today has been perfect."

Dave squeezed her hand. "It really has been, hasn't it? Our first Christmas at the beach house."

Inside, the house welcomed them back with its warmth. The girls shed their snow-damp outer layers and headed straight for the remaining cookies and hot chocolate. Dave rebuilt the fire while Margaret found herself drawn to the desk in the corner where she kept her Beach House Diary.

While her family settled in the living room for one more Christmas movie, Margaret wrote about the day, detailing how the unexpected snow had transformed Cape May into a winter wonder. She described the sledding hill and the spontaneous community they'd found there. Looking up from her writing, she gazed through the frosted window at the snow-covered Victorian homes of their neighborhood, where the Cape May snowflakes continued to fall gently against the darkened sky.

In that moment, watching her family bathed in the amber

light of the fire, hearing their laughter blend with the soft music from the television, Margaret realized they'd created the perfect new tradition. Not the elaborate party she'd initially planned, not the carefully orchestrated holiday moments she'd tried to transplant from their old life, but something entirely new and wonderfully their own.

She wrote one final line in her diary before closing it: "Some Christmas magic can't be planned—it has to find you."

Rising from the desk, she joined her family on the couch, fitting herself into the space they'd left for her. Dave put his arm around her shoulders, and she leaned into him, feeling the rightness of this moment, this place, this new chapter of their lives.

Outside, the world was quiet and still, their beach house Christmas wrapped in a perfect blanket of white under a clear, star-filled sky.

EPILOGUE

It was a warm, balmy April day, the kind that hints at summer without fully committing to it. Margaret stood in the kitchen of the beach house, wiping down counters, while Dave tackled the living room windows. Harper and Abby had been assigned to sweep the porch, though Margaret suspected they were spending more time watching the seagulls than actually sweeping.

"I think we're almost done with the spring cleaning," Margaret called to Dave. "Just in time to enjoy some of this gorgeous weather."

Dave's phone rang, and he pulled it from his pocket, glancing at the screen. "It's Tom," he said, eyebrows raised as he answered. "Hey, Tom, how are you?"

Margaret continued wiping but slowed her pace, watching Dave's expression change as he listened.

"Another one?" Dave said. "That's what, the fourth developer this year?" He leaned against the window frame, nodding occasionally. "Less than Mitchell offered? That doesn't surprise me."

Margaret moved closer, trying to piece together the conversation. Dave caught her eye and gave her a small smile.

"I see," Dave continued. "Well, I appreciate you keeping us in the loop." He paused, listening intently. "Really? You've decided to keep the house and just half an acre?"

Margaret's heart quickened. She and Dave had discussed this possibility months ago, late at night when the girls were asleep. Just idle talk, dreams spun in the darkness. At least, that was what she'd thought.

"That's a fair price, Tom," Dave said, his free hand reaching for Margaret's. "Actually..." He looked at her, a question in his eyes. She didn't hesitate before nodding, a smile spreading across her face. "Actually, Tom, that price works perfectly for us. We've already discussed this. We'd keep the Christmas tree areas managed with help and let the other areas be forested and free for nature and wildlife."

Margaret squeezed Dave's hand, hardly believing what they were doing. But it felt right, completely and utterly right.

"That's great to hear, Tom," Dave said, grinning now. "We want to preserve what makes this place special too."

When Dave finally hung up, Margaret was practically bouncing on her toes. "Are we really doing this? Buying Tom's land?"

"He seemed really pleased with the idea," Dave said. "Said he trusts us more than some developer who'd clear-cut everything. He's going to talk to his real estate attorney and be in touch." He wrapped his arms around her. "Looks like we're going to be preserving a little slice of Cape May."

"The girls are going to be ecstatic," Margaret said. "Remember how they kept talking about how sad they'd be if the Christmas trees were gone?"

"And now they won't be," Dave said. "Tom's keeping his house and the immediate property around it, and we'll manage the rest." He kissed the top of her head. "How does it feel to be a land baron?"

Margaret laughed. "Overwhelming. Exciting. Perfect."

The sound of the girls bickering drifted in from the porch,

breaking the moment. "I should probably go supervise the sweeping situation," Dave said, releasing her.

Margaret nodded, but as soon as Dave stepped outside, she moved to the window overlooking the street. She pushed it open, letting the April breeze flow in, carrying with it the distant sound of ocean waves. The salt air filled her lungs, and she closed her eyes, savoring it.

Summer was approaching rapidly. Soon, the quiet streets would fill with visitors, the beaches would be dotted with colorful umbrellas, and the Washington Street Mall would hum with activity. Their first full summer at the beach house stretched before them with endless possibilities.

She imagined lazy mornings with coffee on the porch, afternoons at the beach building sandcastles with the girls, evening walks for ice cream, and sunset strolls along the shoreline. Dave planned to help the girls improve their boogie boarding skills this year. She pictured them all together in the waves, laughing as the water splashed around them.

They still had their farmhouse in West Cape May and the gardens to maintain, of course. The vegetable beds would need tending, the flower borders would require Margaret's careful attention, plus their farm stand would be opening for the season soon with its bounty of fresh produce and Margaret's preserves. But having this slice of heaven for the weekends was perfect—a beloved retreat that complemented their gardening life, a place to enjoy a different kind of beauty just minutes from their daily routine yet offering its own special magic.

And beyond that, she saw more summers stretching into the future. More holiday gatherings filled with warmth and laughter. More beach house memories being created year after year.

She turned back to the kitchen, a smile playing on her lips. Their beach house adventure was only just beginning.

* * *

Pick up book 18 in the Cape May Series**, Cape May Diamonds,** to follow Margaret, Liz, Dave, and the rest of the bunch.

Start book 1 in my new Ocean City series, **A Summer in Ocean City.**

ABOUT THE AUTHOR

Claudia Vance is a writer of Women's Fiction and Clean Romance. She writes feel good reads that take you to places you'd like visit with characters you'd want to get to know.

She lives with her boyfriend and 2 cats in a charming small town in New Jersey, not too far from the beautiful beach town of Cape May. She worked on television shows and film sets for many years. She's an avid gardener and nature lover.

Copyright © 2025 by Claudia Vance

All rights reserved.

No part of this book may be reproduced in any form or by any electronic or mechanical means, including information storage and retrieval systems, without written permission from the author, except for the use of brief quotations in a book review.

This is a work of fiction. Names, places, events, organizations, characters, and businesses are used in a fictitious manner or the product of the author's imagination.

Made in United States
North Haven, CT
29 August 2025